DREAMS OF REALITY

6-HUBB

DREAMS OF REALITY

Sylvia Hubbard

To order additional copies of this book, contact:
Xlibris Corporation
1-888-7-XLIBRIS
www.Xlibris.com
Orders@Xlibris.com

Contents

To My husband, Calvin,
and our wonderful children:
Magdalenemakaila and Zechariahseraphim.

We are destined to prosperity, Baby,
and as long as we
have each other.
I am yours forever and a day.

Author's Note

This book is a work of fiction. Names, characters, places, and incidents are used fictitiously, and any resemblance to actual person, living or dead, except as noted below, and actual events is entirely coincidental. Some real people and places may appear as actual characters and events in the book to give a sense of historical and reality accuracy, however specific incidents are entirely fictitious and should not be considered real or factual.

Chapter 1

Pulling her gown down, she tried to be comfortable in Dr. Welch's presence. Skye Patterson knew she shouldn't be so uptight. Dr. Welch had been almost a father to her. She had been seeing him since she was eleven. Nervously waiting for his last words to her, she rubbed her neck.

When he was done scribbling on her medical records, signing off on many test completions, he looked up at the young woman he had grown quite close to. "Skye, as always your annual checkup is fine." He scratched something else down. "I've already spoken to Dr. Himes. He's happy to have you as a new patient. I don't want you to worry and he's already suggesting a psychiatrist for those panic attacks we've been unable to cure after all these years."

"It's not your fault. You've done your best. Thank you for the referral, Dr. Welch. I appreciate it."

"My son went to medical school with him before . . . you know. He seems like a fine young man." He changed the subject scratching his salt and pepper scruffier beard. To speak of his son, Edward Welch, Jr. was always difficult. Dr. Welch had not taken his overdose of Ecstasy very well. The entire community of Davenport, Ohio was shocked to hear of Eddie's death; especially his father who had no idea his son was a drug user. He'd had no idea what the drug was or even heard of Ecstasy. Skye had done him the favor of researching the drug and gave him the information. He seemed to take the death even worse, but after a while he healed and went on. "You are going to be fine," he assured her. "This is a huge step for you and I am proud of you." He smiled the most comforting grin up to her.

She nodded nervously licking a full dark pink bottom lip. "I'll be fine." This was said more to reassure herself, then him.

He stood up. "Good. You're going to be fine. It will do you good to get out of Davenport and go somewhere new. Detroit is definitely somewhere new." He pulled the curtain around the table she sat on so she could change. She didn't see his worried expression on his face because she was too busy pondering her own thoughts of moving away from the only city she knew and had matured in. Yes, life had not been easy for her, yet Davenport, Ohio was the only home she knew.

After putting on her clothes, she pulled the curtain away and went to the front desk. Nurse Stephanie smiled brightly handing her a thick medical file. "Dr. Welch said you'd be needing your medical record."

Skye had always thought Nurse Stephanie, since starting five years ago, looked like a Barbie doll with her pretty blonde hair and sparkling blue eyes

"Thank you, Nurse Stephanie." She almost said Barbie. Hurriedly she left out giggling to herself and went to her small black rusted Escort. All her things were already packed in the back. Everything she owned.

Pushing the parking break down with long strong slim fingers tipped with home filed polished nails, she cranked the car up taking a deep breathe. Looking up in the rearview mirror, she stared back at herself. There was fear and apprehension, but a strength she would survive. Going to a new city was not going to be easy. She could get through this new step in her life an even better person from what she was now if she kept her wits about herself.

*   *   *

The female patient screamed again. Dr. Harry Potters frowned as the orderlies held her down while he injected the light pink liquid inside the syringe into her arm.

"No! No! No!" she begged frantically not knowing what else to say to prevent him from giving her the sedative mixed with the drug she desperately needed but knew she shouldn't be having.

All of these patients were becoming more and more aware of their circumstances. Initially the test drug prevented them from remembering, but the more they forgot, the little control the patients had on reality, until the past and present hit them like a smack in the face and the more they realized the drug was doing harm to them, the worst they became because by then they were addicted, but losing all control of mental stability and not being able to stop any of what was going on.

He knew in the end some just died. Some he helped after hearing them whimper in the night like a lost puppy begging for release from the nightmares that would never end. Others became vegetables and sunk into permanent darkness content to be there.

In his mind letting this test subject sleep her life away was the only thing he could do in short of killing her. She will never see reality like it once was because the drugs had taken her mind away.

The present would never be the same for her, but others had come out of the testing just fine. The other three were working like clockwork. A fourth would be better especially now that the price of them had gone up. Five Hundred dollars a session! Fats had ordered another one to become ready soon and Dr. Carter didn't want to let him down. Yet, Dr. Carter was just a Psychiatrist who specialized in the female psychological state of mind looking at this scientific venture only for the money. They never expected a drug like this to really work so well. The tests subjects were already pulling in two thousand a night.

Getting out of there, he took the nearest elevator down to women's gynecology department on the first floor. Dr. Robert Himes was seeing a new patient who possessed the high thyroid level they were looking for. She would be perfect. No parents or social life and passive. One they could mold into whatever they wanted.

*   *   *

Skye had been having incapacitating cramps during her period for the past three months and decided to see the doctor for the pain. She wanted to tell herself the cramps were 'new city' stress. Her account had taken off wonderfully to the point she needed to hire two more home transcribers, Sheila and Margaret, who could take on the overload. Sheila was a retired nurse and enjoyed the extra work. She was able to assist Skye on the account giving her more time off to get moved in and find her way around town.

Dr. Himes was in his late thirties, almond smooth hair with eyes to match. A captivating smile adorned his lips seeming to mesmerize her and he was extremely nice.

"Are you taking any birth control, Ms Patterson?" he asked quite concerned after the examination.

She shook her small oval face confused as to why he would ask such a question. "I-I don't . . ." she stuttered blushing. "So-So I don't."

He patted her knee reassuring she would be all right. "That is understandable, but a single woman living in the big city shouldn't be caught dead without it. Good or bad- anything can happen plus it will regulate and nearly stop your flow so you won't have a sever menstrual cycle."

Anxiety was slowly creeping up around her. "D-did you read my record?" She rubbed the back of her neck. "I mean having s-sexual . . ." She could not breathe.

"Calm down." His tone was firm, but calming. "It's alright. Dr. Welch wouldn't put you in the hands of someone who would do you any harm. Yes, I know you were sexually abused at eleven, Skye, but I'm only assuring myself and you that if something comes up, we are both prepared for it." He firmly gripped her shoulders forcing her to meet his calming brown eyes. "You are my concern. I know you've had it rough, but we must be positive. In a big city like Detroit, it's only natural for you to do this."

She forced herself to calm down. "Alright, I guess I can take it."

"Good." He went to the cabinet. She watched him get a key out of his pocket and pulled out a pre-filled syringe with light pink fluid. She saw more vials with the same colored liquid in them, just before he closed and locked the door replacing the key back in his pocket.

"What exactly is this?" she inquired quite curious.

"This is a new form of birth control that been specially engineered and I've chosen it just for you."

She found those words rather strange. If the birth control seemed so 'special' how did he have the chemical on hand so immediate? Skye kept this concern to herself as he prepared the needle and spoke more about the light pink liquid inside the syringe.

"It's a newer version of Depro-Vera without the side affects. Depro Second Phaze—that's the test name I assure you. I'm including a prescription of Anaprox-DS to cease the sever cramping you have during your period until the birth control can take over. You'll know when this happens. If the cramping continues to bother you, I can prescribe some Darvocet-N100's for you."

Being a medical transcriptionist she knew the effects of these drugs to her system and did not want to go through what other patients she had typed experienced. "I don't think that's necessary." She hated taking drugs, yet he sounded as if he knew what he was talking about and only wanted her to feel better. Relief filled her allowing her trusting nature to come to the surface.

This is a three-month supply I will be injecting in your arm, but I'm going to schedule you to see me in a month and a half to check up on your pain and hopefully progress. If there is soreness in the vagina, it's merely a small convulsing side affect that your body might have from your period being stopped or slowed. A warm bath and lots of water to drink should relieve the uncomfortable sensations. Keep up your vitamin routine increasing your calcium supplement a bit." He pushed her sleeve away, and then he inserted the needle in her skin noting she only gasped a little. "I sincerely do hope the best for you, Skye. If you need to speak to someone, please feel free to contact a colleague of mine, Dr. Ryan Carter. He's extremely good working

with the female psyche and panic attack victims." He passed her a
business card. "You will be fine if you take it easy and try not to work
so hard."

She nodded a little assured. "Maybe I should make an appointment with him? It's not healthy of me to be so apprehensive."

He smiled a beautiful white smile. She'd never saw a Cauca-
sian man with so much whiteness in his teeth. He must have a
good dentist. "Why don't I let my nurse set you up with an appointment tomorrow about ten?"

"That's good for him? So soon?" She had to wonder a bit why
he wanted her to be a priority. If this doctor was so good, he had to
have a long line of patients waiting to see him. Still, she kept this
concern to herself as well.

"He's a friend of mine, of course he won't mind for me. Come
back to the clinic tomorrow. He'll be here."

This made a bit more sense. Dr. Himes was doing this as a
favor to her. Maybe he valued Dr. Welch and decided to put more
dedication into her. She was grateful for it, yet deep down inside
she still wondered what his reasons were for taking care of her and
giving her 'the hookup.' "Thank you, Dr. Himes." She slid off the
table.

"No problem." Leaving her alone, he took a deep breath. Dr.
Potter was standing outside the door.

"How'd it go?" he asked anxiously to his partner.

"Fine. Quite fine. There shouldn't be any problems." They
went to Dr. Himes office to speak more privately.

*　　*　　*

Putting her clothes on she looked over at the mirror behind the door.
With her hair in corn rolled braids all the way down to the middle of
her back, she looked rather plain in the t-shirt and jeans. As angelic as
her oval face was with the crème brown sugar of her flawless smooth
skin, the small nose, and the moist thick lips, she still found it hard to
believe the image that came back to her in the mirror. She was pretty

when she didn't consider the image as her, but she didn't feel pretty. She felt ugly and dirty sometimes as she remembered the gross stench of the foster father's breathe on her neck and the groping hands of the female counselor. Other times she didn't feel anything at all. She was just Skye Patterson, a plain Jane with no middle name who was just trying to type her way through the world until she died. She didn't need any excitement or friends other people craved to get by. She was happy to be with herself. Although loneliness was a bitch sometimes, she typed those feelings away as she had the feelings which came when she thought about her rape.

Driving home in a daze from the day's endeavors, she entered her Westside three bedroom residential home. Two bedrooms were upstairs the master bedroom having its own private bathroom. The lower bedroom on the first floor was being used as her office across from the other bathroom. There was a living room as soon as you entered with the dining room off to the right. The kitchen was in the back of the house and the basement held extra things including her washer/dryer room.

Picking up the paper on her porch on her way in an interesting article on the side bar of the front page caught her eye. Not really the article, but the man in the picture above the article. He was tall, broad shouldered, and extremely handsome. In the article he was being awarded some mayor's plaque and was being honored as a community leader. Her finger rubbed the face on the paper and wondered what it would be like to meet him.

Placing the paper away from her, she shook her head, going straight to her office. She would have a panic attack or throw up from being so nervous.

She rarely went anywhere except her office, where she earned a living as a home transcriptionist. She did medical and word processing, plus light medical billing for a couple of doctor's. Sheila also helped her with this as well. Going straight to her office, she pulled out her dictionary of medical terms. Although she never saw the birth control Dr. Himes had mentioned, she remembered he said the drug was new to the market so she could find some article related to the chemical or the study of the drug on the Internet if she searched hard enough, but at this point, she did not really feel like doing anything. There was a slight soreness in her arm from the shot and she knew she would rather spend the rest of her energy typing rather than concerning herself with a birth control she knew would never be used for sexual means. It was to slow her period down to keep the cramps away. That would be all its use for her—nothing else. She had no intentions of having any sexual relations in the near future and to concern her worries with the birth control would be a pure waste of time.

Instead she turned on her computer to begin typing. Setting her fingertips to the keys relaxed her and listening to other people's problems made her feel less upset about her own isolated lifestyle.

Maybe she would meet someone perchance in fate or something. Maybe she wouldn't have an attack and act a ninny or shy and maybe one-day hell will actually freeze over, pigs will fly, and she'd walk in her bedroom and see Thaddeus Newman sitting there in a nice black robe waiting to make love to her.

Oh yeah . . . not!

Chapter 2

Craig Simpson entered the private entrance avoiding the front desk of the small office of his blood brother, Thaddeus Newman, a meticulous goal oriented young man. They had been friends since childbirth. Born in the same year and their mother's closer than anything, Craig was the brother Thaddeus never had. His older sister, Heather was the exact opposite of Thaddeus who had a calm disposition about everything. Craig had hardly ever seen Thaddeus angry about anything. He may become pique or even bothered, but never screaming mad. Even though Thaddeus had played football all his life until he had torn a major cartilage in his knee in a Rose Bowl Game when he played in college for the University of Michigan. Ruining his football career. He still received a master's in business management and opened up his own real estate redevelopment and construction company. Being a black businessman in an industry filled with other minorities, his success was noted all over the country. He had business ventures in five major cities, but based his business in Detroit, Michigan.

Craig on the other hand had excelled in high school ROTC. After serving eight years in the Army, he joined Detroit's police force becoming a detective in Illegal Operations for the 2nd Precinct.

When he entered the office, Thaddeus was on the phone. Craig caught his light cinnamon eyes and nodded him toward the nearest chair across his desk. Craig waited patiently as the large frame blood brother discussed meeting some potential customers tomorrow at the bookstore café in the strip mall he enjoyed to visit. Once off the phone, he called Trisha, his assistant in the front of the office to enter the appointment in his planner.

"So what's up, Bro?" he asked leaning back in the chair.

Craig could hear the chair protesting the weight and pitied the chair. "My sergeant wants to speak with you. He's waiting in the private entrance. I didn't want to come through the front because I didn't want Trisha to know we were here."

He frowned displeased by this surprised. Thaddeus did not like surprises and his strong fingers drummed irritably on the table clearly showing his upset. Craig never visited him at work, wanting to always keep the knowledge of them being close private to others because of Craig's position and Thaddeus many contacts. Even when he called Thaddeus at work he used Mr. Smith so no one could put two and two together about Thaddeus Newman and Craig Simpson.

"Look Thaddeus if you don't then don't, but I wouldn't ask if this wasn't important to me and the force."

Thaddeus calmed down a bit noting the serious look in Craig's pitch black eyes. "Fine, show the sergeant in." He pressed the button. "Trisha please hold my calls, I'm busy with some paperwork."

"Yes, Mr. Newman," her soft pitch clear diction answered back.

Soon, a gruff looking man entered the office. At 5'10" Sergeant Bill Nolan had a girth that clearly showed he missed no meals.

They shook hands as he sat in the other chair next to Craig amazed at how truly comfortable the chairs were.

Leaning on the desk after everyone sat down, Thaddeus said, "Alright Sergeant Nolan, what is it you want from me?"

Sergeant Nolan decided not to mince words with this large young man. He had been a fan of his football season, and to sit in front of him now was almost an honor. He got right down to business. "Most of what we have to go on about this case is speculation and from leads, taps, and street sources. Trevor Coleman Sr. a.k.a. Cole Forsythe better known as Fats, has been in the underground business for about five years or more. He literally corners the drug market in the Metro Detroit Area. One of the most popular drugs, which have been the bulk of his wealth, has been GHB, the popular date rape drug. He controls the market in distribution, but this of course is only hearsay. Last year, we tracked him to Venezuela, where we suspected him of buying steroids, then to Chatham in Canada, here our agents assumed he was stocking up on the party drug, Ecstasy. We have gathered supposed evidence of his Internet commerce, where we believe he is buying key ingredients for GHB. We track him down, arrest him, and have to release him at least ten times in the past twelve months, while our prosecutor's charge him."

"Until recently, no Michigan State Police chemist knew how to test for gamma hydroxybutryate, which is what GHB stands for. He's done his operations so well, we are having a tough time finding out if he does have any connections to these crimes and it's no field testing of GHB on the street, so when his people who are connected to him, or even Fats himself is caught with the drug, or ingredients to make GHB we can't fully charge him until the lab results come back, which won't be until two to three months from now. The more we wait for the prosecution, the little our case will weigh against his lecherous attorneys."

"Fats and other wealthy crime bosses in other cities are donating large sums of money into private non-profit scientific research of late, on neuron-chemicals that may affect the brain. He uses his import/export business as a front to do his underground dealings and money laundering."

"This is all word of mouth, right? Because if you had proof of this we wouldn't be here discussing this." Thaddeus questioned.

Craig nodded a bit frustrated. "We've been on the case for about four years and we can't make anything stick to him or his organization. Initially, Fats was heavily into prostitution, but it's becoming ever increasingly hard to track down all his women when he isn't getting them off the streets."

"Call girls?" Thaddeus suspected out loud.

"You could say that . . ." Craig said rather evasively. "From my resources, he's gotten a way to take everyday women and control them at a level of subconscious behavior where these women have no idea what they are doing."

"This is all hearsay and I'm suppose to prove it?"

"Yes and no." Craig knew Thaddeus would catch on quickly. "You see we know Fats have been using his connections approaching well-to-do gentlemen for services. Most have denied. Others when we've approached them have not been acceptable to the situation. We've decided two things: either find a john to testify or find a prostitute we can get to testify and identify the major players who are helping Fats."

"Or both," Thaddeus concluded.

"You understand where we are coming from then, Mr. Newman?" Sergeant Nolan smiled relieved.

"Most definitely. You want me to be a john and get a legitimate solicitation from him, then see if I can investigate the girl?" Outwardly, he seemed uncomfortable about the idea.

"Yes, except we need you to just prod the girl for information and we will do the investigation." Sergeant Nolan said statically.

He frowned something fierce enough to put fear into anyone who didn't know him well enough. Thaddeus seemed quite displeased at the fact Craig would even consider him.

"Trust me, Mr. Newman, we wouldn't approach a man of your position in the community if we didn't think Fats would be highly interested in you. You'd be a great contact and he'd be positively gullible to your every request."

"Which is?"

"Before we get into details we need to know if you are willing to do this."

Thaddeus rubbed his hands together slowly deep in thought. "So I would be requesting the service of a woman for . . ."

"A night of course."

"And would have to . . . perform?"

"No of course not. You'd have two choices: talk or we can provide you with a sleep-induced agent, which we believe has only a raggedness side effect to the chemical we believe she could be taking. Meaning she'd awake with a hangover or grogginess."

"And how many sessions would this require?"

"Four to five. Once a week. Maybe even less. We want to first try to get information out of her. When Fats feel things are going well, the contact we have at his side now, can go in with a wiretap and discuss the arrangements he has with you. We'll have the discussion on tape and we can hold him on solicitation of prostitution. We need some substantial way to retain him so he won't flee the country, which we feel he might do if he knows we are too close. We will draw a sample of her blood. She of course will be asleep. Once we establish we won't need her anymore or she doesn't test positive for the GHB substance, we will leave her alone."

"Throw her to the curb?"

"Sort of. Hopefully when this is all over, if the drug we suspect they've given her really does what we've heard, she won't be mentally disturbed. We do ask that you be careful and remember the woman probably does not know what she is doing."

"How does the drug control anyone? I must know."

"It easily controls a female when you do in-depth study of the female psyche, but we haven't discovered the details to this. We're obtaining our own Neuro-Psychologist soon, then we can all better understand exactly what is going on with these women."

He nodded. "I will help."

Craig sighed relieved. "You won't regret it. The precinct is willing to agree to take all responsibilities so any individuals won't sue you."

"Well that's reassuring." His tone was surly.

The sergeant pulled out an envelope. "We've set up an apartment at the River Place Towers in Downtown. We'd like you to reside there because we've rigged the apartment already with special microphones. Now we know and understand your privacy and we respect it. There is a green button on the bottom of the remote which mutes the room you are in, but we do request you leave this on at all times when having any discussions with the woman. Especially when you're trying to get information from her."

Thaddeus nodded understanding while Craig relaxed a little more. He didn't think Thaddeus would be at all susceptible to the idea.

"This envelope contains the different keys you need for your apartment—each one labeled, the legal papers we'd like you to drop in the mail and the first payment we know Fats will probably request. Don't negotiate, accept his terms."

"How will I meet him?"

"The inside contact will tell Fats you're interesting in unique entertainment. You're wealthy single and just looking for a little fun every Saturday. Someone you don't have to scope for and someone you don't want to share. You're willing to pay heavy for it if he can give you what you like."

"What will I like?"

"That's up to you. We prefer requesting the same girl and we hope the first one pleases you."

He looked at Craig. "Do you think the contact could relay this? Pick out a good one?"

"He could do all the arrangements for you, and I can guarantee you will like what you see."

He shrugged it off as if the woman didn't matter. "Fine. When is the first meeting? This Saturday?"

Sergeant Nolan shook his head. "No. Give us a week to get the ball rolling, but we would like you to move in by tomorrow. If need be, any of your numbers can be switched or rerouted on a moments notice."

"This should not be problem. My mobile phone and pager are usually my real numbers outside the office."

"Good." He stood up. "Craig will be our go to man, but we suggest waiting until he makes contact with you. If perchance the police happen to take you in on solicitation and we aren't around, ask for Mr. Aggie Smith as your public defender. Never contact him or I unless there is a life-threatening situation of not the 911 kind could understand."

Thaddeus again nodded his understanding of the matter. "It was never my intention to speak to Craig again."

Craig knew Thad was kidding, but only because he'd known him for so long. A man of his size and girth should not go around with a frown on his face.

"Well if there is nothing else," Craig said breaking the supposed tension giving his blood brother a look of disgruntlement. "Your contact name is Pooh."

"Like the bear?" Thaddeus asked sarcastically amused watching them leave the office and squeezing a stress ball tightly.

Standing outside of Newman Enterprises waiting for an elevator to go to the parking structure, Craig chuckled. Sergeant Nolan gave him a skeptical look. "What do you think he will do to her?" the sergeant asked once they were enclosed alone in the elevator.

"Fuck her."

He gave Craig a hard look. "You are kidding me?"

"Hah. He'll try to fight it. He'll even deny it's happening, but the man probably needs the outlet."

"So why didn't you want me to let him know any criminal activity by him will be dropped?"

"And not see him killing himself over breaking the law?" he asked fighting to keep a straight face, but he couldn't for long and broke into laughter.

The sergeant didn't find anything funny because although Craig knew his blood brother well, he didn't, and knowing that the young man would be highly upset didn't sit too well on his conscious, but he would trust the chap wouldn't come after him. If Thaddeus did decide to go after Craig Nolan though, that would suit him and a couple of boys at the precinct just fine. Craig had pissed a lot of people off on the force with his loud mouth, sarcastic remarks, and arrogant attitude. The young detective probably needed a good beat down for a change.

Sergeant Nolan didn't think Craig would be able to withstand a tackle from Thaddeus, although the young man's demeanor would not suggest he could ever get that violent for no just cause. Thaddeus' college days were quite well known to collegiate football fans. He had a great season before the last game that ended his career as a defensive lineman. He could get to a quarterback faster than lightening and people had clearly known he'd probably be second pick in the up-coming draft season.

Yet people were still proud of him. He had come back and

made a real estate redevelopment business into a multimillion-dollar business then expanded to construction. Already he'd received several government and private contracts this year and Fortune magazine predicted by the end of the year his business would be worth over a hundred million dollars with the casino deal he had struck with MGM Grand and Motor City Casino.

Yes, the young man would be a success and when this was all over he would be a hero to the city of Detroit. Wiping out Fats would be a great asset to many community groups since his corrupt operations within them would be shut down.

Chapter 3

She awoke instantly and looked at the clock. It was nine in the morning. Jumping out of bed, she ran to the bathroom and washed up. The appointment with Dr. Ryan Carter was in twenty minutes. This was a catastrophe. Damn her for staying up late to work and take her hair out of the corned rolled braids.

In five minutes she was washed up. As she brushed her teeth she yanked her honey brown shoulder length hair straight then put it in a ponytail.

After e-mailing her work to her clients she rushed off to the clinic, arriving ten minutes late.

Dr. Carter was waiting in the room for her and seemed too glad to see her. He wasn't cute as Dr. Himes, but his tall "Michael J. Fox" appearance made her a little uncomfortable especially the way his green eyes were sizing her up from head to toe as if recording her measurements and size.

They made quick introductions. He had read her charts from prior psychiatrist. Immediately, he asked her to speak about her feeling concerning her rape and how she would feel now if she ever becomes involved sexually or emotionally with a man.

"I really don't know how I feel right now. I don't think about what happened to me in the past any more in details only as a moment that happened. What happened was so long ago and seems so far away I don't questions the when's or whys." Taking a deep breath she made the cutest twinge of her nose deep in thought. "I don't involve myself with anyone right now, not because I'm afraid or anything. I mean, I had acquaintances, friends, and sorts, but living here I'm working all the time and I've been enclosed in my new house I've just gotten.

My only contacts are my e-mails from my employees and associates on the web."

He nodded. "How have your sexual relations been?"

"None. I-I haven't um . . ." She cleared her throat feeling her heart rate increase. "I don't have any."

"Why is that?"

She began to rub the back of her neck nervously feeling a panic attack surfacing. "No reason. I-I mean they say I'm healthy physically, but I don't engage because I haven't been . . . attracted, you could say, to anyone."

"What holds attraction for you?"

She closed her eyes remembering the picture of Thaddeus Newman. "A strong face and personality. Self strength more than anything attracts me."

"You are beautiful. I am surprised men have not approached you."

"They do and have. I just don't talk much except for business. I don't know why, but just the idea of talking with them and engaging in personal conversations give me panic attacks."

"Panic attacks?" he questioned scribbling on his pad.

Skye nodded. "Sever panic attacks. It's like when I'm not conversing with them face to face on a personal level I'm fine. Some of my clients are men and I have no problem speaking business, but as soon as it gets personal, I can't concentrate. My pulse races and I feel trapped.

"You have tried drugs?"

"Yes, but they only made me sleepy or annoyed. I hated feeling the way they made me feel and I hate taking drugs of any kind in general."

"Even if they made the attacks lessen?"

"Even then. The idea of being dependent upon a chemical makes me feel weak and I don't like feeling like that emotionally not when every day it feels like a struggle to get by naturally for me. I tried them all and I didn't like that. I did have a dog and that helped a lot when I went out in public, but she died a year ago and I just never got another one because losing something felt awful and I didn't want to lose another one. I have an easier time going out in public and having Shelby helped me make this decision to come to Detroit. If she had not been in my life, I wouldn't have had the inner strength to move here by myself. I know once I get over her death, I'll get another puppy, but right now, I have my work to keep me busy and a new house to finish up."

"Have you tried hypnosis?"

She shook her head. "What on earth could that accomplish?"

"A lot of things. The sound of the male voice changes and for some reason when a tone of interest in you comes, your mind immediately begins to panic and sends signals to your body in a negative form."

She shrugged. "I'm always open to suggestions."

He stood up and pulled out a beautiful emerald on a long gold string. She smiled at the beauty of the penny size green gem. "I want you to relax, Ms Patterson, then slowly watch the gem." His voice was quite relaxed as the emerald moved slowly left to right in front of her beautiful lavender eyes.

Skye felt her body relaxing as she heeded his instructions. She felt light as a feather than total blackness surrounded her and nothing for a long period of time. Her whole body gave a sense of being lifted and in the distant a strange ringing of the phone fought to invade the tranquil darkness. Fading into the silence, there seemed to be a deep calming voice speaking to her from far away, but as much as she strained she couldn't make out what exactly the voice was saying. She decided to relax and listen to the voice wondering if she was experiencing a memory of her childhood and the voice was her father talking to her when she was a baby. The thought of this made her happy. Since she was little she always carried the knowledge it had not been her father who had given her up, but her mother, and he probably didn't know she existed. He would come for her one day, she always wished and when he did he would have the most enchanting deep voice just like the one she could barely hear.

When she came to she was still in the same chair and he was leaning back in his chair putting the emerald in his inside jacket pocket. Blinking her eyes, adjusting to the light, she took a quick check of herself. She felt and looked fine, yet her mental state had somehow been affected. She couldn't explain exactly what was affected.

"How do you feel?" he asked yet a bit triumphant.

"Calm. Notable no different." She didn't want to express she felt as if someone had told her a secret, but she couldn't remember what had been told to her.

A soft bell chimed behind her. He stood up. "I do recommend you come next week, Ms Patterson. I'd like to see how you've done."

"I would too." She gathered her things. "I'll make an appointment."

He seemed quite pleased. Too pleased in her opinion, but she pushed this thought away thinking it was just her mind being apprehension of everything and everyone.

Leaving out, she sat in her car in a rather thoughtful mood feeling quite strange.

Looking at the time she didn't feel an hour had passed since she had walked in his office.

She was free for the rest of the day and decided to go to a nearby strip mall near her home to get her shopping done. The experience was a calm one until she stepped outside the store. Near the grocery store was a café. Being a nice August day, many people sat outside.

What drew her attention was the large built man. Shoulders! The broad expansive shoulders from behind drew her notice. There were several other men sitting with him, but none of them seemed to catch her eyes except him. Even his deep laughter made her eardrums tingle.

Sitting at a table right behind him, she listened quietly. A waitress walked up to her and asked for her order. She told her club soda because she didn't drink coffee and even though tea would have been more appropriate, she didn't want to get hyped up about now.

"Mr. Thaddeus Newman," a waiter called quietly near the front of the café doors holding a cordless phone.

The man she had been watching raised a strong hand with long clean pedicure fingers. The deep timbre of his voice made goose bumps appear on her arms. How could a man so large be so elusively seductive and not know it?

He excused himself turning to the young man carrying the phone, which was right near her. She hurriedly stood up trying to turn anywhere except facing Thaddeus Newman terrified of her reaction if he looked at her with those sensual brown eyes she remembered in the newspaper. In her haste she bumped the waitress carrying her club soda spilling the drink all over them and then rushing away leaving one of her bags of groceries.

Sitting in the safety of her car, she almost passed out. Her panic attack was quite sever. No, the hypnosis had not work! She'd promptly tell Dr. Carter next week. Closing her eyes to calm herself down, she thought about Shelby and how the settler use to know when she was having an attack and rub her arm or legs. Her body began to relax and her breathing slowed down.

Someone tapped on her window; she screeched in shocked startled by the large shadow. Looking up she saw the black Adonis she'd just been admiring holding her grocery bag.

Lord no, she thought frantically dreading as she got out the car using the car door as a barrier between the two of them.

Thaddeus waited patiently as she reluctantly opened the door and stepped out. She seemed homely, frail, and quiet. He was use to awe and adoring looks from women, but she reacted as if she wanted no part of him or his interest. Purposely she didn't make eye contact by putting on dark sunglasses before standing out the car she snatched beside her driver's chair. He handed her the bag which she quickly took giving him a quiet thanks.

"You left your groceries at the table," he explained wishing he could see her eyes through those dark glasses wondering what she was thinking and feeling. He was trying to make conversation. "I assured the waitress I would make sure you got them."

"Thank you," she said again hurriedly putting the bag in the cars back seat. She was screaming for her mind to stay calm and the only way to do this was not to make eye contact, but his proximity unnerved her and damn if he didn't smell good. Lord, the man smelled delicious.

Though he'd gotten a message to meet his contact soon, this young lady somehow held his interest. If she would probably just make eye contact from behind those dark shades then . . . maybe he wouldn't be so interested. "My name's Thaddeus." He held out his hand to shake.

She pretended not to see the outstretched hand and began to get back in the car. "H-Have a nice day, sir." She closed the door cranked the car and drove away as quickly as her old black escort would allow her to go.

He sighed chalking this up as just one of those episodes in his life that just couldn't be explained. She seemed interested in him, but didn't want to go ahead with what she felt. Or he was feeling for the first time in his life rejection from a woman?

Either way he was not going to let the mysterious plain young woman bother him. He was on his way to meet Pooh at the apartment downtown.

As he was about to step towards his car, a yellow business card on the ground caught his attention. Patterson Transcription Service—for all your transcribing needs, 'The Skye's the limit!' It was rather odd, but the card looked freshly dropped and he was positive the owner was the young woman. Tucking the card directly in his wallet he decided to investigate her further on a later date if he remembered. The whole ordeal with her had been a rather humbling experience or maybe he was just losing his touch.

Chuckling to himself, Thaddeus decided to call Trish en route to downtown to start an immediate search into the transcription business. If the investigation turned up no lead to this mysterious "no interest" woman, he told himself he could chalk it up as two ships passing in the night. Yet, funny how he wished he didn't want her to just pass by.

*   *   *

When Skye finally pulled in her driveway, she screamed to herself. How could she be so stupid and act so silly? He was just a man. Nothing more. Maybe it would have been a great business contact? No he was in real estate. Still networking never hurt any business, she knew this and she was not about to let her stupid little idiosyncrasies come between her business, which she so enjoyed.

*   *   *

Getting to the apartment, he passed the keys of his black Jag to the valet and went into the complex. This was only his second time there since moving his things in last night. It felt weird calling something home, since he lived basically at a hotel for the past three months. He had moved out of his home about that time giving up his space to his sister and her low-income bringing home husband. Giving up his home had been a decision that he had come up with when he knew he could not take another moment of Heather badgering him about being single and setting him up every night for dinner with one of her money hungry girlfriends. He was almost glad to move out, but he had never had time to find another home. Being an entrepreneur and single gave him no time for his personal life. He knew if he was married with a supportive wife, he would be able to accomplish a lot more networking with old friends and acquaintances, but he knew with the crowds he went around most women regarded him as their ticket to never working another day in their life and he didn't want that. He needed a woman in his life that would continue to do what she did if it made her happy or given the opportunity: find out what she loved to do and have a goal.

He really cared nothing about any woman other than his sister and mother in his life about now. Heather could be quite difficult in her temperament. She was spoiled and selfish since another father raised her and not their own. Their father left their mother when Heather was four, but Henry Newman was a nice caring man. An encouraging man that had raised Anne Pitman's children like his own since he had none.

Anne and Henry lived in Florida now and his mother called him every once in a while to keep in touch. Heather stayed in Detroit because of her husband's job at the new casino. She tried many times to get cash from her only brother, but Thaddeus tried not to let his sibling get to him. There was only so much you could do to help family, but he was not willing to go broke supporting grown people.

Sitting down on the comfortable leather couch, he reached into his blazer pocket and pulled out the card that the woman dropped when she had gotten out the car. He'd never needed transcription service and why he wanted it all of a sudden was a mystery to him. Trisha took care of everything so why should he be so interested? Yet when he told Trisha about inquiring of a transcription service she seemed rather agreeable.

The buzzer sounded for him to answer the door. A skinny young man stood in the hallway with a cigarette hanging on his bottom lip. "I'm Pooh. You Tad?"

Thaddeus frowned at the Ebonic talking man, but knew this was his contact and would have to put up with the ignorant young man. "Come in. Would you like something to drink?"

"Hell yeah! Oh man, this is fly!" Pooh began to look around uninvited to do so. Thaddeus said nothing, but watched him with his peripheral vision. "Oh hell yeah!" he shouted when he entered the bedroom. Thaddeus smiled because he had thought the same thing and he was positive Craig had something to do with the setup of the exceedingly expensive seductive bedroom. The bed had to be a double king size from its enormity and the black furnishing added just masculine touches around the room. He brought the man a gin and tonic.

"This place will be the tops on my list for my next place. I didn't know the River Place had it like this."

"So why does Fats say?"

"He says he wants to meet you. You gotta go to the Network Wednesday morning at seven. He'll be there. That ain't one of his places, but he's got contacts that frequent there and helps him get business done."

"What about the girl?"

"I ain't seen no one, because Fats don't want to do nothing until he meets with you."

Thaddeus really didn't want to do something like that. To meet the man himself seemed quite dangerous, but he didn't think Fats would want to do business with him until he met him. "I'll do it, but it's got to be at nine. Can you do that?"

"Can you old timer? Too early for you, huh. Make sure you take your vitamins." He gulped down the drink. "That'd be no problem." He tapped him on his arm. "I gots your back, 'kay? I told Fats 'bout what you wanted. Fresh as a new day, and no sharing. You want top dollar. Right?"

Thaddeus nodded. "Top dollar," he agreed.

Pooh handed him the glass. "Don't worry, you'll get what you want man. When I told Fats you were interested in a little fun every Saturday night, he lit up like a Christmas tree. I know he's gonna want to do it. He just needs to see if I'm not fucking him over. So you bettah show up or dat's my ass, man."

Thaddeus only nodded again as he ushered Pooh out the door. The slang the young man spoke made his head hurt trying to decipher. He would put a good diction qualification if this language was on the street now, for the girl he wanted.

*　　*　　*

She sat up abruptly in bed. Something strange had just happened. The digital clock beside her bed read seven in the morning. She could tell that daylight savings time was coming in effect, because the sun seemed to just crest the horizon making longer nights, so why didn't she feel rested? Going into the bathroom she splashed cold water on her face, then stared up in the mirror back at herself.

Her dark lavender slanted eyes were extraordinarily expressive even when she could not say what was on her mind.

The dream. She had a dream.

For some people this seemed normal, but she had not dreamed since . . . since the rape. It was like something in her brain died and she thought a part of her had, until last night when she was standing in a strange office next to two other women. One lady was truly frightened and Skye comforted her telling her everything was okay, but she doubted these words even as she spoke them. A door opened and a heavyset man and a man in the early sixties walked in. The fat man seemed doubtful and whispered something to the other man. The other man coaxed him on, and she heard something like, ". . . won't remember a thing."

Skye stepped forward as the two men approached them. The heavy set man looked her over like she was some sort of meat product. "Is there a problem?" she asked.

The heavy set man looked over at the other man not sure if he should speak his mind.

"Go ahead and speak. She is not aware, so speak sensibly."

The heavy set man met her eyes with beady black eyes of his own that chilled her to the bone. She didn't like the vibes she received when she looked at him. His voice was decrepitly calm. This bothered her too. "No problem, Skye. Do you know why you're here?"

She shook her head suddenly not at all feeling well. "I don't dream. I don't dream. Is this a dream?"

The older man came fourth and held her shoulders. "Close your eyes Skye and listen to my voice."

She started shaking and her heart rate increased. She didn't want to be here. She wanted to wake up. "L-let me wake up," she begged.

"No Skye you can't. You must stay. Please stay."

"M-make the bad man go, and I will stay," she promised.

"He's gone," the older gentleman said. "Now relax. Stay calm."

She calmed herself down. Controlling her panic attacks was

becoming easier and easier. He helped her to a chair and comforted her more. She really didn't need or want his attention, but
allowed him to do so since comforting her seemed to relax him
too. She knew she was somehow important to these men for some
reason, but had never met them a day in her life. This was strange.
No one dreamed of people they never met.

Before she realize it she was sleeping in his arms

That's when she awoke in her bed. The man had been telling
her something, but for the life of her she couldn't remember. She
knew his voice was still pounding in her ear when she awoke, but
even that faded away.

The clock had read four in the morning and she had still been
sleepy. Drawing the covers closer to her she surmised the experience must have been something she saw on television that she had
not remembered.

Skye wiped her face once more and replaced the towel. 'Something on television.' This seemed reasonable to assume, yet the
reasoning didn't sit well with her. Still she was not going to dwell
on this now. She had a busy day ahead of her.

Little did she know this was the first step into a reality she
would never forget.

Chapter 4

Dr. Roth Powers came in the conference room with an assuredness of his own. Thaddeus watched him closely as he sat down between Sergeant Nolan and Craig. The sergeant thanked him for coming on such short notice.

"We want to move fast on this," Craig explained, "But we need an understanding of what exactly is going on. Mr. Newman is going to be the one dealing with the subject, and he wants to take precaution while helping us out."

"Indeed," Dr. Powers's gruff voice said. He had dark ebony skin, which contrasted severely with his thick rim white glasses. "I was a intern of Dr. Potter's about twenty years ago. He was just getting into mind controlling drugs for the government on his own, but he found out he could make a lot more money doing research on his own with private investors. I went with him of course because I knew this was a genius that would eventually discover something great at the rate he was going. When GHB was discovered about ten years ago that is when I left the project. By this time Dr. Carter had come aboard and was also an expert at mind controlling substance yet only dealing with the female psyche. With ingenuity they managed to perfect a new drug that can be mixed with Depro-Vera and used to take the mind to a sublevel of consciousness unbeknown to the test subject. Subjects with high-level thyroids are perfect. When used in patients with normal to low levels hallucinations occur severely depending on the low level of thyroid. The perfect subject though will in time accept these as dreams if they are not too sever and mentally negative. The better they are taken care of during this time that the brain is 'dreaming', the better they fare when they awake. We believe Dr. Carter perfected the method of hypnotizing these women and making them do what he wanted them to do when he wanted them to do it. Dr. Potter stays on the project to make sure the well being of the subject is taken care of correctly when she is in the sub-level conscious state of mind."

"Why women?" Thaddeus asked.

"Because they are more docile and would more or less take it. When given to men whether they had a high thyroid level or not, they immediately became violent in and out of the dreams." He continued, "When you interact with this individual make her experience with you pleasant. If she protest or becomes upset you must relax her and make her feel comfortable. Get her to take her mind off the fact that this is a dream that she can't control and she can't wake up from. It's frightening for her and you need to do whatever it takes not to cause any mental strain on her so that she will enjoy the time you need her at these moments."

Thaddeus looked at Craig who seemed almost too delighted with this situation for Thaddeus. He didn't realize that he had a frown on his face that was making the Sergeant and the doctor uncomfortably nervous about involving him on this project.

"Are you sure you want to involve yourself on this case, Mr. Newman?" Dr. Powers asked nervously not at all liking how grim the young man was looking. "I'm sure a more patient person for this project would be suitable."

"Oh no," Craig said trying to keep his laughter from bubbling. "Thaddeus is a most patient man. Boundless if you ask me."

Dr. Powers raised a brow in disbelief. "Then there should be no problem." He looked at the Sergeant. "May I have a word with you privately?"

When they were gone, Thaddeus looked viciously at Craig. "What the hell are you trying to pull?"

"Nothing," Craig said innocently. "I am just merely assuring them you would be perfect. I think you can handle a little gentleness."

"To a woman I've never met?"

"You've got to remember Thaddeus she's probably just a regular woman. Nothing out of the ordinary than what we would see everyday. I know that this will be difficult and you can pull out any time before we even start this."

"Oh yeah. What would Fats think when I don't show up tomorrow?"

"He'd think you just changed your mind. It would all be understandable. I would understand."

"Fine-"

"Wait!" Craig stood up in protest.

"Ah ha, didn't think I'd pull your card." This time it was Thaddeus turn to laugh, which he did quite openly leaning back in the chair. Looking at his watch, he stood up. "I have to go, but I assure you, I wouldn't pull out. I know you've got something up your sleeve Bro, but I haven't figured it out yet. I just hope you aren't thinking I'm just going to see this broad and know I can do anything I want and take it. You know I'm not like that and just can't sleep with anyone. What's the use of a woman if her mind is not there? I have no idea what this woman is like and I know I won't be attracted to her in the least bit so your plan to hook me up won't work, Bro."

"What makes you think in any way I want you to do anything to this poor unsuspecting woman?"

"Because for the last two years you've tried to hook me up with every woman you thought was nice, but it turned out she had an ulterior motive and I saw right through her facade. Now if you'll excuse me I have an appointment with some clients. I still have a business to run."

Craig watched him leave and cursed under his breath. How the hell had he figured out so much in so short of time? He'd be right. Thaddeus wouldn't be able to resist her.

Chapter 5

Another disappointing session with Dr. Carter and Skye was still unsatisfied. He asked her in depth about her feelings for Thaddeus Newman when she confessed she was thinking about him after seeing him in the newspapers and the other day. She was confused about how she felt about him.

"I guess you could call it a crush. I guess?" She was doubtful. "I don't understand it. I like the way he was looking that day and in the newspaper. And he smelled . . ." She closed her eyes remembering him being so close and the more she thought about the more she noticed about him. The nice shape of his head, the strong nose, chiseled chin, thick neck, and of course the shoulders. Broad, bullock shoulders that made a woman want to rest her thighs on.

"Excuse me?" Dr. Carter asked.

She realized she had been describing him out loud and blushed.

"Don't be embarrassed. I am glad you are taking some interest in men. That is a positive sign for you considering your hardship."

"My hardship? I don't think my rape at a young age could ruin my chances for an emotional relation with a man, should it? I don't want it to. I accept the fact that it wasn't my fault and I know it will forever be in the back of my mind, but I hope my panic attacks would go away eventually."

"Quite possibly. Yes, you maybe attracted to this man, but anything towards sex would probably make you turn against him. If you met him, and he regarded you with mutual interest would you have sex with him?"

Her eyes were doubtful, but interested. "I would like to, I guess," she said doubtfully. "I'd have to know him personally. I can't—"

"If you were in a situation where there were no restrictions, no consequences, no repercussions would you?"

"I think I would." Just the thought of it made her heart race. "I think I'd tell myself that my panic attacks weren't there. It's just excitement and I could believe it for just one night or two if I knew I'd never have to wake up and see that it wasn't real. That he didn't have any real sexual feelings for me, but I could just accept him, physically and mentally. I don't think reality likes me, so if I knew it wasn't real I could handle him."

Dr. Carter seemed pleased with her answer. This bothered her to know he felt comfortable with what she said, because what she said had not made her comfortable. To know to only deal reasonably with Thaddeus Newman in dreams was not a very comforting thought. She wanted to be able to deal with him at all times. That was healthy. What she wanted was not healthy in her mind, but decided not to express this to Dr. Carter.

"But I don't dream when I sleep, so I know it will never happen." She added with great disappointed, but retracted this when she remembered just the other day she had dreamed. "Although I did dream the other day."

"You did? About what?"

She related the dream to him and how she had felt afterwards. "I let it passed because I figured with all the changes going on in my life, it must be a positive sign."

He looked rather triumphant. "This could be symbolized as a big step in your life. The old free spirited Skye could be emerging, the one that's not afraid of changes and new experiences."

She shrugged still feeling depressed, but glad her hour was up. Leaving the Woman's clinic, Skye got in her car and drove to her appointment at Newman Steel. Trisha Galvin had called a couple of days after Skye's meeting Thaddeus Newman, leaving a message on her answering machine. She was intrigued with the business wanting to know more about what Newman Steel did and why her services would be beneficial to them.

When she arrived to meet Trisha she was surprised to see the woman was as old as she at twenty-two and looking quite friendly with her large features. "I'm Trisha Galvin, Mr. Newman's assistant. It's nice to meet you. I've spoken to your references you gave and they are quite pleased with your work. I'm delighted to say we've accepted your contract terms and willing to work with you." Trisha led her to a huge richly decorated executive conference room that looked about as big as her entire house. It seated about twenty-five nicely with the most comfortable chairs she'd ever seen. "Have a seat please." She pointed to a chair near the end of the table.

Skye tried not to sound nervous when she asked, "Mr. Newman will be present?"

"He's not scheduled."

"Can I ask how you heard of my service? I usually pass my card out and solicit mainly to the medical fields and such."

"I received your card from a friend." She didn't say the friend was Thaddeus, but the woman was too sincere not to sound tricky. "Mr. Newman has large contracts and I am usually in charge of typing them." She sat across from Skye with an interesting look on her face.

Skye knew she would like working with Trisha. She was quite nice and honest when she spoke.

"With more and more contracts proposed to Mr. Newman it is becoming quite tedious for me to keep up with my typing duties and still be his assistant. Your services would be appreciated in this area. What I need to know from you is if you had any experience with contractual work?"

"Mostly on a medical basis and I know how government contracts are. I'm sure with normals and samples I can adjust. I'd like to do an example for practice and just so you can see if I do understand."

"That can be arranged. I have templates of many of them on my computer and I can give you several examples. Mr. Newman's wordings are quite simple to pick up and most times he transcribes on micro cassette."

"So is contract work all I will be required to type?"

"Maybe letters and proposals. This and that. I will make sure there aren't any surprises."

Skye looked relieved. "I am just honored you chose me. Mr. Newman's company is quite successful and I do find something different a challenge."

"Now I would like to discuss prices."

Skye reached in her brief and pulled out her price sheet she used regularly for customers. Just as she was about to pass it to Trisha, the double doors to the conference room opened and Skye felt she couldn't breathe. He walked in looking just as sexy in a dark gray Verace' suit as he did the other day. Good Lord, he wasn't scheduled! Control yourself, Skye, she ordered herself.

"Mr. Newman," Trisha said looking surprised. "I thought you wouldn't be here?"

"I was finished with Mr. Blake and decided to work during lunch at the office. Lyn told me you were still meeting with Ms Patterson." He looked at her now and outstretched his hand. "How do you do, Ms Patterson?"

She stood up and shook his hand. If she just put on professional heirs she would be able to handle herself and not vomit. "Hello." Her tone was stiff and monotonous.

"We've met before haven't we?" He leaned forward so she was forced to meet his eyes.

"Yes. We have." She stepped back on purpose not wanting to be in his proximity for long. Deliberately avoiding his eyes was hard without being outright rude. She put on her reading glasses to give him the allure she actually needed them to see, therefore giving her the opportunity to get away from him, and not make complete eye contact.

He frowned which she thought it was because he couldn't remember. Of course he wouldn't. Quickly she explained. "In the parking lot the other day. I dropped my grocery bag and you brought it to me. I appreciate it."

"Anytime. Please have a seat." He sat down beside her at the end of the table. "I wasn't frowning about that though," because he was faking the whole thing. He knew perfectly well where he had met her he just wanted to make sure she remembered him. Yet her eyes still showed no interest towards him. Matter of fact, she looked at Trisha with more interest than she did him. It was like how he looked didn't matter at all. "I noticed your eyes are different."

It was her turn to frown. "Different, sir?"

"Mr. Newman, please," he corrected her. "Yes, different. I've never met a woman of our color with purple eyes."

"Elizabeth Taylor has purple eyes, but I don't consider mine purple. They are more like a blue with a hue when the light reflects upon them. I assume one of my parents had this color eyes, but I never met them so I wouldn't know."

"An orphan?" he questioned. "All alone in the world, are you?"

She nodded, picking up his 'alone' connotation. Did he really want to know of her martial status or did he just show this sensual concern for all women as part of his playboy style? Skye convinced herself she would not fall for it, no mater how much her senses screamed he was the most gorgeous man in creation. "I am truly comfortable with it, are you?" She snipped

"I am quite comfortable with it. My father left me when I was young, but my mother was quite supportive. Yet enough about us, let's get down to business." He picked up the price list she had. "These are mostly medical report pricing?"

She nodded. "I have only done service with medical companies, Mr. Newman. My regular price per page is two dollars and per line is eleven cents."

He sat back in the chair. She winced hearing the plastic creak in protest from his weight. "Well Trisha pointed out that we use a smaller font size and it would adjust the page line wouldn't it?"

"Yes it would give me more lines per page, but I am willing to adjust-" She kind of had a feeling he would be cheap!

"No need. Matter of fact, I was willing to charge thirty cents per line to compensate you. I don't think our lines matter, but it's the size of the documents. On contracts I insist you charge that amount and for proposals and letters I insist you charge twenty cents a line."

"But-" She was in dubiously shocked. He wasn't cheap; he was wasteful! No one in their right mind would pay those exurban prices.

"I insist."

She shut her mouth. The man was charging way too much, but he didn't want to listen.

"Do you accept my terms, Ms Patterson?"

"I guess I have no choice in the matter since you insist. I would like it on record I protested."

"It will be noted," Trisha cut in feeling the tension between the two of them. "With that settled why don't I show you around, Ms Patterson, while Mr. Newman gets that agreement on my desk for you to sign."

"Please do." She was eager to get out of his presence and stood up hastily. He stood at the same time outstretching his hand. He noticed she shook his hand with a lot of caution, as if he were a rattlesnake about to strike.

"It was nice to meet you again, Ms Patterson." He tried to sound deeply sincere to put her mind at ease.

"Feelings mutual, Mr. Newman. Good day." She followed Trisha out the office, who happily showed her around Newman Enterprises.

When the tour was over, she had Skye sign the agreement and then Trisha gave her a copy of the agreement along with the templates and examples. After Skye was on her way, with a promise to Trisha to have the sample e-mailed by tomorrow morning, Trisha went into Thaddeus office to see him staring out the window thoughtfully from his chair. Immediately she knew the man had leave of his senses once she realize he was daydreaming. Thaddeus Newman never daydreamed!

"Can I be honest, Mr. Newman?" she asked standing in front of the desk.

He didn't bother to turn around to address her. "You know I value your honesty, Trish, go ahead."

"As long as I've known you, I've never known you to make someone so uncomfortable as you did, Ms Patterson. Was this deliberate?"

"Did I make her uncomfortable?" He looked concerned as he turned to look at her.

Now she knew something was wrong with him. All the incidences abruptly came to her, as a wicked smile crossed her face.

"What?" he asked seeing the glow in her eyes.

"You like her."

"I don't," he immediately responded.

"Oh no. It's worse than like, you love her!" she exclaimed. "I never thought . . . I mean . . ." She paced as she spoke giddy with excitement. "Your lifestyle, the way you've stayed away from women . . . I thought your work involvement was because you wanted your company to succeed, then even after you succeeded you still worked hard, which confused me, but it was front. It was all to protect you from women, wasn't it, but she's different and you see this, right?"

He squinted in anger. She had figured it out to the bone. Thaddeus relaxed his features and sat back in his chair feeling defeated. Trisha knowing his feelings really didn't matter to him. He knew she would never tell anyone about how he felt, but was what he felt really love? How could this be? Lust he would believe, but Skye was so unlike anyone he ever knew.

"I can't explain it. I met her at the café I go to all the time when I want a light atmosphere for the clients. She left her bag and I just couldn't help myself. At first I saw a plain Jane, then I saw something else. Not on the outside, but there was something on the inside. A reservation about me."

Trisha twisted her wide nose at him. "Not every woman is attracted to you."

"The majority find me appealing. I am a modest fellow, but I know my looks don't curdle milk. My height alone draws attention."

"Maybe it's your height that scares her. She might not like tall men."

"She looked right through me Trish. You received more attention than me."

Trisha saw that this had hurt his feelings. "I might rephrase that. She may just not like your type. Too cute you know."

"No I don't know."

"Sometimes women feel that a man who is powerful, successful, and handsome, such as you, is too much for them."

His tone dripped with sarcasm as he said, "So I should be weak, broke, and ugly, then I'm sure to get the girl, huh?"

She smiled sympathetically amused. To see him struggling with these new emotions was quite amusing. This man had control unending, yet one woman seemed to unravel him. "Just not so forward, sir. She seems rather shy. If you push your interest too much, she might turn away."

He realized Skye had some apprehension about him, but he wanted her attention and felt she should feel the same way. "So I should let her come to me, but at the same time make my interest known a little at a time. I don't want to play games with her, Trisha. I am not like that."

"In order to help her get over her shyness and express her interest in you, you must sir. If what you feel is true and it's not a one-time thing for either one of you, then you must give her time. Things of this nature cannot be rushed."

"So I have to play around until she likes me?"

"Oh there is no doubt she finds you attractive. You forgot I was watching as you two spoke and the look of admiration was in her eyes several times when you weren't looking. I think her control of her emotions is even more perfect than yours."

"Should I find that a compliment?"

"Almost." She sat down in the chair in front of his desk. "You should know every woman wants a man who is successful, powerful, good-looking and strong. Not just on the outside, but the inside too. You have to step back and make her realize she wants you just as much as you want her."

"So what should be my next move, Trisha?"

"I think you should wait."

"For what?"

"You've outstretched your hand, now it's time for her to take it. Right about now, she knows that she was deliberately called here because of you. This was no coincidence encounter. You've made your interest known to her, now you must wait until she does the same. Can you wait that long?"

Lyn from the switchboard buzzed in. "Mr. Newman, there is a Ms Skye Patterson on the line. She wanted to speak to Trisha, but she isn't at her desk, so I thought you might want to speak to her. She's on line four."

His smile was clearly triumphant as he looked up at Trisha who had a surprise look on her face. "Thank you Lyn, I will pick it up."

"Why do I think you planned this?" she asked suspiciously.

"Because I did." He pressed the pick up line using the speaker indicating for Trisha to be quiet. "How may I help you, Ms Patterson?"

Skye was hesitant to answer. "Y-You may have forgotten to sign the agreement."

"You think I may have?" he questioned. "And how did you come to this conclusion?"

"Because when I looked at the end of the contract once I got home, it wasn't signed by you or Trisha."

"Then we must get this resolved. How about . . . tomorrow I swing by and sign the contract."

"Swing by where?"

"Your residence. I believe you are a home contractor aren't you?"

"Yes, but there's no need for that, Mr. Newman. I can just return to the office."

"Well, I might not be here tomorrow. Matter of fact my sched\ules quite filled tomorrow. How about you meet me at the café about three? I should be finished with my appointment there."

"Can't Trisha sign it?"

"No I would rather I sign it. Trisha may be my assistant, and can conduct some of my business, but I do still run the company."

"Of course. So tomorrow at three at the café?" she confirmed controlling the disappointment. "Goodbye Mr. Newman." She seemed too happy to get off the phone with him.

"Till tomorrow, Ms Patterson."

When he turned off the speakerphone, Trisha asked, "why do I have the feeling that you didn't sign that on purpose?"

"On purpose. Deliberately and if she would have contacted you first I would have already told you she would have been calling and insist that I sign it."

Trisha giggled. "I like how you think, Mr. Newman."

"I like how you think, Trisha."

"I'll remember that when bonus time comes around." She stood up. "You are going to heed my advice aren't you sir?"

"Of course. Take it slow if I don't want to lose her."

Chapter 6

Arriving at the Network, he was surprised to see it open with a large bodyguard standing in front. It was usually closed before the noon hour, but of course Fats had connections and Thaddeus wouldn't be surprised if he had his hand in the profit pot as well. Coming here had thrown a monkey wrench in the police plan to get Fats on solicitation for now. The back up plan was to get another operative in with today's meeting to hopefully take pictures of the deal without anyone knowing. Thaddeus wondered if they had succeeded as he entered the darkly lit club. Music played loudly, but no one else seemed to be around except Fats' people. A beautiful scantily dressed woman met him at the door as he entered.

"Mr. Newman?" the woman questioned looking him up and down as if he was her last meal.

"I'm here to see Fats."

"Come on dis way. He been waitin' for'yr." She ushered him to a platform where Fats sat on a couch with another scantily clad beautiful woman. Five large men were strategically placed around Fats, which Thaddeus assumed were bodyguards. He noticed the bulges at the sides of them and knew this was no joking matter. No matter how large he was a bullet could take him out like a bitch. One of them approached him and patted him down.

Fats explained. "A usual procedure for a man in my position."

Thaddeus was glad he wasn't asked to carry a wire because he was sure that was what the man was feeling for. "Perfectly understandable."

"It's so good to see you, Mr. Newman." Fats didn't get up, but nudged the woman beside him out the way. She stood up giving Thaddeus an appreciative glance. "Later Thelma," Fats barked. "Please sit, Mr. Newman, or can I call you Tad."

"Mr. Newman is fine." He lowered himself on the couch next to Fats who was pretty large, but with a custom tailored suit on.

"I didn't believe one damn word Pooh said when he came saying some rich cat was looking for a good time. Is it true?"

"I am a man of wealth and finding suitable women to suffice a need has become quite tedious. I want the pleasure without all the promises, if you know what I mean. To do it legitimately has become a nuisance. Money is all I'm willing to give and they usually want more than I can buy. Emotions, marriage, a baby, you know."

"I understand. I am a man who enjoys a good fuck every once in a while with no strings attached too."

"I would like pleasure more than once in a while. If I'm displeased with your first choice, I will let you know. I'd like a somewhat educated woman who I can relate to verbally and physically. I am willing to pay a high price for monogamy as well. I don't like to share."

This sparked a blood-curdling greedy smile on Fats' face. "That would be a lovely price. A five figure initial fee and four figures continuously. I have to make up the money I would be losing to do this."

"I am willing to pay."

One of the women delivered two vodka and club soda drinks to them setting the tray on a small table in front of the couch. She gave Thaddeus another appreciative glance.

"This can all be arranged."

"I know it can. You are Fats and everyone knows that you can do anything you want." Thaddeus raised the glass up. "To a good relationship."

"A good union. This is a prosperous union for me, Mr. Newman."

Thaddeus gulped the drink down and winced only a tiny bit as it burned his throat. "So I can expect her this Saturday?"

"At ten at night on the dot." He passed Thaddeus a napkin with some writing on it.

Thaddeus looked at the napkin, but made no change in expression as he read $10,000 initially and $2000 a night. This was the expected fee. Pooh had given Craig a tentative price of $20,000 which had been placed in the envelope the sergeant had initially given Thaddeus.

Thaddeus put the napkin on the table, and then reached inside his coat to pull out two envelopes. "This should cover me for the first five nights."

One bodyguard picked up the money, and another picked up the napkin. Thaddeus saw him ignite the end of the napkin with a lighter and drop the flaming paper in an ashtray.

"Why don't you stay a while, Newman? My girls would make it worth your while."

Thaddeus looked over to see the two women dancing sexy together rubbing up against each other giving him a "come-join-us" look. Standing up, he straightened his jacket and sighed with disappointment. "Unfortunately, I have so many appointments today, but I do appreciate the offer. Maybe if I am dissatisfied with what you initially offer me, I can come back and get a sample." He winked in jesting.

"Anytime for the right price, Newman."

They shook hands before Thaddeus left. He didn't feel at all right about paying for sex. He'd never had to in his life and now that he had the experience under his belt, he felt completely turned off to the woman he was going to meet Saturday. He pondered the thought that if it was Skye Patterson, maybe he could get his libido up a little.

Arriving at the café a quarter to three, he was shocked to see Skye sitting there sipping on water. She was tapping the glass rather nervously.

"Have you been waiting long?" he asked sitting down across from her.

"No, not really," she lied. Skye had been there since two. When she was sitting at home waiting for three, she couldn't concentrate. "Surprisingly the café outside is still open."

"Yes, usually about this time of year in Detroit it's cooler. You're from Davenport, Ohio?"

"Yes."

"My mother had family in Akron. I believe an aunt and cousin, but when my aunt died the cousin moved south. So you have anyone in Davenport as far as family?"

"Actually I was raised in an orphanage outside of Chicago. I was adopted at two by Mr. And Mrs. James Patterson who already had two children—a boy and baby girl. They died in a car fire and we were all separated when I was seven. I moved from so many homes until about eleven when I was molested by one of the foster parents. I ran away, ending up in Austin, Ohio about an hour drive from Cleveland. Again I was put in foster homes in Davenport moving from family to family until I was sixteen when I applied to the courts for independence. I was a pretty good typist and making a living quite profitably as one."

"Do you plan to type all your life?" he asked.

"No. I do plan to retire in a few years. I've invested my money seriously. One of my foster parents was an investment broker and I learned early what the profits to long term investing could do. I plan to have two million by the time I'm thirty five."

"Exactly how old are you now, Ms Patterson, if I may be so bold to ask?"

"Twenty—two."

"No children?"

"None that I know of."

He chuckled getting the joke.

"And you Mr. Newman?"

"No children."

She flushed. "That's not what I meant. I meant how old are you?"

"I will be thirty next week."

"So why isn't a man of your type married?" she delved out of curiosity. He was too good to be true.

He frowned taking offense remembering what Trisha was saying the type of guy Skye thought he was. "What type of man am I?"

"The type that should have been hooked by now. The good fish never stay in the water long."

"The smart fish do."

"True and I must say you are quite intelligent, Mr. Newman. I read on the Internet just how intelligent you are." She frowned this time. "Your business keeps you quite involved and away from your personal life."

"I believe I have some personal life or I wouldn't be here speaking with you."

With that note, she clearly became put out. Reaching down into her brief, she pulled out the contract. "Here is the contract for you to sign. I wouldn't want to make you late for any of your other appointments. I know you're a busy man."

He wanted to say, "not to busy for you," but he knew that would be forward. Even when he made a small indication of his interest in her, she seem to become turned off, yet she made this effort to be here on time—hell early. What the hell could he do to her to show some interest in him? It was frustrating.

Skye could sense he was suddenly irate about something, but she would not ask even though she did want to know why. Watching him scratch his name on the last page, curiosity was killing her to know what had made him so upset. "Is there a problem, Mr. Newman?"

"Yes," he said sharply. "I want to know why when our conversation becomes personal, you get more colder than ice."

She gasped at his frankness, and then she huffed more to herself. "Was I? Have I?" Sighing she sipped her water. "My experiences with men have not been pleasant, Mr. Newman, but that's neither here nor there. You are my client and I wouldn't dare want to change our relationship. So when our verbal banter gets too personal I tend to freeze up as you say. I can't help it. You must excuse me, but in any way think I don't enjoy talking with you." She tried changing the subject slightly. "I can see why you choose this café. It's relaxing here and you don't seem so threatening."

"Threatening?" he asked wanting her to elaborate on that.

"Well your size does make a difference when people speak to you."

"I don't consider me that large."

"Of course you don't."

He leaned on the table. "Can I have your hand?"

Nervously she reached across the table. He unrolled her long slim fingers with the real nails unpolished on top of his open palm. He placed his other hand in hers turning them up until they were palm to palm. Her heart raced at his touch and she had to take deep long breathes to control the pounding in her chest. "I am human, just like you, with the same skin, blood, and bodily organs. I feel, hurt, and love the way you do. My hands are no different than yours. Matter of fact, your fingers are probably ten times stronger than mine."

She smiled at his teasing. "But your size-"

"It's nothing. I'm not a violent person, Ms Patterson. Do you think I am?"

"I don't know you well enough to agree with that."

He held her hand in his. "Then you need to get to know me. Good day."

Skye watched him walk away and decided if Thaddeus Newman did show up in a bedroom naked she would probably jump his bones. He was the most sensual man she had ever seen or met. She wanted him, but she knew there was no way she would ever convince him to want her in return. He probably found her a joke. One more to add to his many conquests. Although, she wouldn't mind being his conquest either.

'Oh please,' she huffed to herself. Even if he were lying naked in front of her in her bedroom, she wouldn't take the chance of doing anything. She couldn't take the pain in her heart, because then she knew she would be truly in love with him.

Chapter 7

Saturday was a normal day for her. She did her usual schedule. Shopping, running errands, paying bills, and sorts. At six she cooked a nice baked salmon, rice and corn, then retired to *Sleepless in Seattle* at eight. By nine Skye was in a deep sleep when a strange ringing emitted from the phone.

*   *   *

Soft music played and candlelight surrounded the front room and bedroom. He paced nervously as he occasionally watched the clock. 9:55pm and no one had yet to drive up. Taking off his jacket he moved to the bedroom. The instructions given to him just this morning by Pooh said he was supposed to light the room by candlelight and leave the front door unlock. His gift would be there on the dot.

Going into the bathroom he decided to freshen up, then just lie down and wait. Just as he finished he heard someone in the other room. Stepping out the bathroom, he noticed the lights were out and only the five candles lit the room. Dressed in a sensuous red see-through ankle length silk gown, with a dark red robe, was the most sensuous woman he had ever seen in his life. The lighting made the details in her face hard to determine, yet the simple beauty beheld his interest enough of what he could see as he walked close to her. Her hair was down to her shoulders with a bit of a curl slightly to give a voluptuous look. She was made up with a medium touch of make-up. With the most sensuous swaying of her slim hips she walked close to him from the bed. Each move deliberate in drawing his attention to her. This was a woman consumed with getting the right response from him at each moment. Every fluid movement was designed to heighten and capture pleasurable responses from his body and mind. She was a dream come true to him, now if only he could get Skye off his mind when he was with "the case", he would actually enjoy the entire encounter.

"Am I dreaming?" she asked tenderly cupping his face in the palm of her hand as if he would disappear. She had read his mind. When his head leaned into her sweet smelling palm, he heard her softly exhale softly. No, he felt so real. "I hope I don't wake up when we get to the good part," she teased.

Pulling her close, he smiled brilliantly. If he spoke he might wake up himself. When she pressed herself against him, he felt himself instantly become aroused. He never was affected in this way from any woman. She was definitely a dream. The most beautiful dream he could ever envisioned. Slowly their bodies rocked to the music. She turned around so her back could press tightly against his chest and his arms wrapped around her waist. Yet as much as he found himself attracted to this mysterious woman, he still wished she was Skye. His infatuation with the homely typist confused him. Thaddeus knew he was out of his mind to want something so bad. He had to keep his head together. Skye could never be one of these girls. There was no way she would know what to do. What felt strange was even though he could hardly remember her features, except those exquisite hued eyes, it was her personality that attracted him. It was as if she knew the inner most of his own psyche and she could be the woman he always wanted, but he didn't know why he thought this. What if this young woman was his Skye? Did he think he could control himself?

Enough about what he wanted, he needed to concentrate on the now and right now she was doing her best to seduce him into making love to her. This woman, as Craig had said did not know what she was doing and when this night was over she wouldn't remember anything. It would have all been a dream to her and then what? He didn't know. All he knew right now was that she was rubbing wantonly against him and if he didn't stop her, he wouldn't be responsible for his actions. Did she realize how wanton she was becoming?

No she didn't. The doctor had said this was her subconscious doing this and what those goons had put in her body and head. What drug had they used? What had they told her? He had to know.

"Did they tell you to do this to me?" he whispered softly in her ear hoping the microphones picked this up. Spinning her around then rolling her up in his arms, he pulled her close as they swayed close to the music.

"They told me to come up here to this room lay on the bed and wait for you to touch me."

"Who told you?"

"The voices."

"Do you know their names? How do they look?"

She didn't want to think about the horrible man with the beady black eyes. The one that made her scared. She was sure to awake from this wonderful dream and what she was feeling felt so good and so right. The frustration became evident in her face. She reached up and cupped his face again tried to pull his face close to hers, but he deliberately avoided her kiss knowing if he started he wouldn't be able to stop himself.

She closed her eyes knowing if she didn't give him what he wanted she would not get what she wanted and that was he. Yes, she wanted Thaddeus Newman badly. Her body told her and her mind was in agreement. She had never wanted something or someone this bad and since this dream felt so real she knew she was capable of doing anything with him right now "where there were no restrictions, no consequences, no repercussions." Exactly like Dr. Carter had said. "Just the voices," she answered him in a coarse whisper not wanting to wake up from the sexual torment she was feeling all over her body. "They took me to some office again and this lady with Chinese eyes put all this on me, telling me I was going to have fun tonight and to relax and stay calm, then they brought me here in a black van and said they would be back for me at dawn."

Thaddeus decided not to push it, knowing she was in a delicate state. "Then why did you come up to me if you were told to lay on the bed and wait for me?"

"I knew it was a dream when I saw you. I had to act upon the moment. Do you hate me for that?" she worried.

"No, I could never hate you. You are a dream to me." His lips lightly brushed against her teasing her inner core that rippled with pleasure. He heard her purr at the new sensations he stirred within her and smiled to himself. He did enjoy pleasing if she made sounds like that. Forcing himself to keep his mind on his objective, he whispered in her ear, "Where are your from? What is your name?"

Too many questions. He was trying to make her think and she didn't want to think. Rubbing her body against his, she desperately tried to distract him. Thaddeus knew if she continued to massage against him, it would not be long before he would succumb to her wishes. He had to be crazy to resist an opportunity like this, but the doctor's words were repeating in his head. She didn't know what she was doing. She would not remember any of this come morning and it would not help his effort in getting to her when she was herself if he ever had the opportunity to meet this woman, which he wanted to know more about as well.

He looked around the room for the remote, which laid on the bedside table nearby so he knew if need be he could get privacy. "Do you think you're in a dream now?"

"Yes. I am. I know in reality I could never have you."

"Why is that so?"

She was quiet. Her eyes looked away from him in a blank stare, then she looked back at him. "No more questions," she pleaded. "I don't want to think anymore. I just want to feel you make love to me."

"Let's have something to drink. You wait here, I will be right back." Reluctantly he released her and went to the kitchen. The glasses he had prepared earlier were still cold. In the right glass there was the serum to make her go to sleep. He had a choice, but he knew if he acted upon his lustful intentions he could never really get what he wanted in the end. What about next time?

Thaddeus would not think about that. He would have to do this tonight and not think about what would happen next time. Grabbing the glasses he went back in the room. She laid on the bed, the robe was off at the end and he could see the beautiful silky olive skin beneath the see-through gown begging for his touch. Sitting up as he came to the bed, she began to unbutton his shirt. By the time he handed her the glass, she was kissing his neck moving her tongue down his neck to his collarbone, and then moving back up again to behind his ear. He couldn't help suc-cumbing as her soft moist lips came back across his cheek to meet with his. The blood rushed through his veins as he gripped her shoulders and deepened the kiss, letting his tongue intertwine with hers. She moaned wantonly savoring the manly taste of him. It was her first kiss, albeit a dream, yet it felt more real than any-thing she could ever imagine. She wanted this dream to last forever.

When he pulled away breathlessly, their eyes met. Thaddeus was shocked to see his smoldering passion mirrored in her eyes turning him on more. She gulped the drink down, before he pulled her in another deep kiss.

He was about to burst as he pushed the straps off her arms. Breaking the kiss, he lingered at her neck, orally caressed her ear loving the way she tightened up and purred even louder making her whole body vibrate with earth rippling sensations, then abruptly her body went relaxed and her breath deepened. Thaddeus looked up to see that she was sleep. The serum had worked that fast. 'Dammit! That was not suppose to happen,' he cursed.

In truth nothing before the serum was suppose to happen, but he didn't expect her to arouse him as much as she had.

After blowing out the candles, he undressed and laid down still needing her nearness for his own sanity. She snuggled up against him. He didn't know what to do, but relax and go to sleep too, yet he cherished her presence. Thaddeus was not use to sharing his bed with anyone, yet he felt so comfortable knowing she was here with him.

Whispering in her ear, "Be mine."

She chuckled softly in her sleep and responded, "all yours."

The thought was extremely frustrating to not know if she meant that or not.

*   *   *

"Be mine . . ." echoed in her brain the next morning as her eyes popped open. Looking around frantically, she saw she was in her bed, not some candle lit bedroom.

The bedside neon clock read 6:02am. It was early, but it felt like she had not slept a wink. Getting up, she went to the bathroom and without turning on the light she washed up. Going to her computer she put her headphones on, turned on her computer and began to type. Along with the new work she had gotten from Newman Enterprise, she still had to keep up her other accounts. This was not difficult with Sheila and Margaret's help, but taking on new work gave her little time on her hobby, which was the basis of her retirement fund.

After about three hours of typing, she decided to take a break. E-mailing her reports in, she made coffee for herself, and then put out two pork steaks for dinner. Just as she was coming out the kitchen the phone rang.

Answering, she was surprised to hear Trisha's voice on the other end. Today was Sunday and usually no clients ever called.

"Mr. Newman dropped off five tapes of a proposal and I'm kind of in a bind. Do you do rushes? We just found out the deadline is tomorrow at three?"

"Of course. Do you want me to come get the tapes?"

"Well, I'm driving around now, I can come drop them off."

Skye gave her the address and directions, and then took two

more pork steaks out. When Trisha arrived she noticed the hag-
gard appearance on Skye's face.

"Someone didn't sleep well, did they?" Trisha teased with caution not sure of Skye's mood.

"Actually," Skye said, "I don't feel like I did. I'm not usually
restless."

"Well I do appreciate you doing this for me."

"Why don't you stay for dinner? I rarely have guest. Matter of
fact, you are the first at my new home."

"I am honored."

Between working on the proposal, Skye cooked. Even Trisha
went to the kitchen a couple of times to stir something or take
something out the oven. By ten that night, they had finished and
decided to sit down at the dining room table and eat.

"Mr. Newman will be so pleased. What do you charge for rushes?"

"This is a first for your account."

"He said to pay you whatever you requested." She took out
the copy of Skye's price list. "The usual proposal is about ten dollars when we add the extras and sorts, so how about fifty. Same day
rushes should be greatly compensated."

"Does Mr. Newman plan to make me a rich woman with his
account alone?"

"Whatever Mr. Newman plans to do, I have no control over
it." She changed the subject. "You are a great cook."

Skye flushed not use to compliments. "Thank you. It might
be from all those cooking shows I watch."

"You should definitely invite Mr. Newman over to taste some
of this."

"Oh really? As if a man in his position would accept."

"He loves good home cooking. His mother never was one to
cook. He came over my mother's home one Thanksgiving and it
was quite interesting to watch a grown man indulge so much. He
was like a kid in a candy store."

"Mr. Newman gets invited to the mayor's house, or even the
governor's house for dinner. Not a little plain typist home."

"You'd be surprised. He would accept."

"I doubt it, plus he's a client. I don't invite clients to my home."

"I'm part of the client."

"You work for him. That really doesn't count, plus I kind of enjoy your company. Trust me, I don't have a lot of friends. Matter of fact, you're my first in Detroit."

"You're a nice girl, Skye. Why are you so alone?"

"To be honest? I'm afraid of disappointment. I guess growing up in places that never gave me what I needed made me so independent. I use to wish for a doll, but I never got it until I got a newspaper route and bought it myself. People use to tell me I couldn't get things or they'd promise me things just to shut me up. I got use to the disappointment, and promised myself that I would just not want things from other people."

"That included friendship and love didn't it?"

Skye nodded solemnly. "I don't think I could take disappointment in my life back then, but now that I'm not in Davenport anymore, I'm finding that I do need friends and even more. Does that sound strange?"

Trisha shook her head earnestly. "It doesn't make you weak Skye. I think that is what you are afraid of. The fact you know what you need in order to make you happy makes you a stronger person. You'll pick good friends because you've waited so long to get them."

"Did anyone ever tell you your second calling was a psychiatrist?"

Trisha laughed. "No, but my mom says I have a good outlook when it comes to people problems. Unfortunately I don't use my own advice."

Skye stretched, feeling the soreness in her back still feeling the grogginess from this morning all over her body. "So you aren't married?"

"I will be getting married next month. He's a great guy and he doesn't mind my long hours of work, which I enjoy."

"That's the kind of guy I like."

"What other qualities are you looking for?"

Skye thought for a second. "I don't know, the usual ones. Thoughtful, sincere, honest. It's so many and I know for sure I'd be disappointed in that department."

"What about Mr. Newman?"

Skye blushed all over and began to protest, but Trisha interrupted her. "I saw the way you were looking at him when he wasn't looking. You can't tell me there isn't interest there."

"Alright, there is, but I don't think it will be reciprocated. That man could have any woman in the city. Heck the state if he wanted to, so there would be no reason to choose me."

"You aren't as bad as you think, Skye. You're quite extraordinary if you ask me. As long as I've known Mr. Newman, he's not been attracted to ordinary woman, yet the women who do seem extraordinary usually are fake. When I say ordinary women I mean the kind who have the nerve to tell him they intend to use him for his looks or money. You are the genuine article and I think in a way he sees this, but is hesitant about expressing his feelings. You should at least try. What's the worst that could happen? He just says no and then what? Life goes on. You'll be a rich woman."

"Well this isn't exactly how I make all my money."

"It isn't?"

Skye shook her head getting up from the table and going to a bookcase in her living room. Trisha followed close behind her watching as she pulled out a small romance book. Handing it to Trisha she asked, "Do you read these?"

"Yes. I love these books and I love Sybil Howard. She's great and I've read all ten of her novels. You hardly meet a woman who can express the black woman's anguish in love situations. Do you read her?"

Skye shook her head. "I write her."

"You what?" Trisha's big brown eyes grew large as saucers.

"I write her," she repeated again. "It started four years ago. I guess I was frustrated about myself as a woman. I was afraid to express my feelings toward men I liked, but in the back of my mind I would make love to them. So I begin to write about how I could meet Mr. Right and soon my writing grew book lengths and my doctor, Dr. Welch, said instead of just writing for myself, I should let others read it. I took a chance. My manuscript was accepted by an Internet publisher, which also printed paperback upon demand. I couldn't believe it and they asked me to write another one. All the money I've earned I've reinvested in stocks and bonds. I use the transcription money to pay the bills."

"Oh that is just fascinating. I would never guess you were Sybil Howard."

"You wouldn't? Heck sometimes I can't believe I've written about these things myself. I had to research extensively to understanding true lovemaking—if you know what I mean—because I've never been with a man intimately, so it was real difficult, but I based it all on my imagination, which I find that I have a lot of." She mumbled under her breathe, "Especially of late" then resumed what she was saying a little louder, "I learned a lot about myself writing these books and I think writing made me overcome my rape. I know making love isn't bad, I just can't find a man like the one I've imagined to really satisfy me mentally and not just physically—although that wouldn't be a hindrance on his part either."

Trisha was really impressed. "I just can't believe it. Promise when you come by the office tomorrow you'll sign my books?"

Skye smiled honored. "I promise, but why would I be coming by the office?"

"To drop off the tapes I forgot then to invite Mr. Newman out to dinner."

"Are you still on that trip, girl?"

"Yes. Just ask. You might be surprised."

Skye huffed in amusement rolling her bluish eyes heavenwards. Trisha was playing cupid and Skye could see she enjoyed it, but she didn't see that Skye and Thaddeus Newman would never be an item. He was too different and so was she.

Trisha began to gather her things up and Skye gave her a disk of the work. After Trisha was gone she worked about three more hours on her other account, before going to her bedroom.

Immediately she noticed some black markings on her pillow. Inspecting the pillowcase closely, she was confused about the identity of the black markings. Going into the bathroom, she noticed there were some more black markings on her washcloth. It was makeup.

But she didn't wear dark makeup. Only lipstick. Going to her dresser she looked at the mascara she hardly ever touched. Opening the bottle she saw the brush was dry and hard. So how had make up gotten on her pillow.

That was the same question she was asking Dr. Carter when she went to therapy the next day.

He gave her several suggestions, but none of them hit the mark. "It bothers me a lot."

"So not only were you exhausted Sunday morning, but you'd somehow put makeup on your pillow and washcloth?"

"No I'd put makeup on my face, but I don't know how or when."

"Have you experienced a sleep walking experience before?"

She perked up. "No. No I haven't. I don't dream, so I know I don't sleep walk."

"But you said you awoke remembering something . . ." he read his notes. "Be mine? Is that it?"

She nodded. "I've still never known anyone to put make up on when they are asleep."

"Maybe you rubbed it on your face in your sleep and since you paid no attention that morning you didn't notice that you'd done so until late that night."

The possibility didn't sit with Skye to well, but she decided to take Dr. Carter's advice until she figured it out on her own. True, she could have had a sleep walking experience, but she doubted it even included trying to put make up on which she didn't possess. That was too strange, but she could not disprove anything yet and didn't want to until she had other proof.

*   *   *

After the session Skye decided to go by Newman Enterprises and Trisha was glad to see her, except that Mr. Newman had left on his appointment downtown. Skye tried to seem upset, but she was a bit relieved. It was much too soon to invite him to dinner.

She went home from there to do more work. When a couple of hours passed she found her mind could not stay on her work. She gradually started just blanking out. Getting her mind off everything, she decided to wash clothes. Separating the colored clothes from the whites, she began to imagine her next book, and then a scent assailed her.

She reached down in the clothes again and picked up a red nightgown. She remembered buying it in Davenport loving the feel of the fabric against her skin. Pulling the gown to her nose, she closed her eyes. *Masculine* was the first word that came to her mind. So familiar . . .

'How . . . ?' This questioned terrified her. Her heart began to race as she dropped the gown and raced upstairs to her bedroom. Smelling her pillow and blanket there was no trace of the masculinity on the sheets. No trace of him. Should she feel so disappointed?

Yet how had his scent gotten on her robe? She wanted to call Dr. Carter really bad. He probably didn't make house calls. This idea made her giggle to herself. She wouldn't think about it. It was probably just some weird problem she had with her senses. It could be the drugs.

Going back online she wrote to several medical companies about the birth control she had received. She even went into several medical chat rooms, but no one was able to give her the quick response she needed. It was four in the morning before she laid down to go to sleep, but her body could only relax. Her mind was too uptight to actually sleep. At seven, she went into the kitchen to fix her some coffee. She had a feeling it was going to be a long day.

Chapter 8

Thaddeus went on as if nothing happened. If he worked harder he didn't think about it. Trisha was oddly quiet about everything too, but he wasn't concerned.

About five in the afternoon, he received a note from Craig to meet him at a restaurant about a forty-five minute drive from Detroit. Thaddeus sent the courier back with a note to cancel. He really wasn't in the mood to see anyone.

"I'm getting ready to go, Mr. Newman," Trisha said at the door only peaking her head in.

He nodded. "Have a good night."

She stepped in not at all liking his attitude. "I've rescheduled your eight am to three, because of your doctor's appointment. Dr. Hoffman called me personally and told me not to let you reschedule again. You are overdue for an annual by three months and he wants to check your blood pressure."

"Thank you."

"Is there something wrong sir?"

"Nothing I can't fix, you know that." He was trying to make light of the situation, but decided that wasn't the route to take, instead he changed the subject. "How are your wedding plans coming along?"

"Fine. The big day is almost here. I've already scheduled you to be there and I've trained Lyn on my duties pretty much that it shouldn't be a problem while I'm on my honeymoon. With Ms Patterson working your letters and such, you should be fine when I'm gone."

"I don't think I've ever met your fiancé."

"Oh I know you've been so busy and he doesn't like visiting me on the job."

"Well, we're going to have to arrange for me to see him one day before the wedding. How about I treat you to dinner?"

"That seems fine. I thought maybe a home cooked meal would be so much better."

He perked up for this idea. "That would be excellent. At your mother's?"

She laughed. "I'll see what I can squeeze into your calendar. Have a good night sir."

When she was gone, he returned to his pondering. Another knock came to his door.

"Thad, it's me," a soft voice came.

At first he thought it was Skye, but disappointment set in quickly as Nicole Anderson peeked in. Stepping in the office closing the door, Nicole looked quite well. Being a fashion model, she was downright gorgeous and with a flair for life unlike Thaddeus. She knew what she wanted in life when it came to the personal side, but Thaddeus thought it had been too much for him. After six months of going steady, Nicole was ready for marriage and had begun to make plans behind his back. Matter of fact, she had decided to tell him on their intentions one month away from the date. He couldn't believe her audacity, and it infuriated him to know she went so far in planning for a marriage he had never asked for. He broke off the relationship and decided he needed a rest.

"How's it going, Thad?" she asked.

He tried to look happy to see her, but conquering a smile for her sake was too difficult. His lips gave a grim look. "Fine. How have you been?"

"Perfect. I just thought to stop by because of your birthday."

"It's not until this Saturday."

"I know, but unfortunately I will be in Paris and I don't think I will be back in the states on time." She stealthily moved to the desk and slid on a corner near him. "I thought we could celebrate early."

"'I thought not. I'm busy."

She looked around the dimly lit office seeing there was nothing in front of him such as paperwork or even a file folder. His desk was clean and she could have sworn when she peeked in before saying something he had been daydreaming. Her tone became annoyed. "Busy doing what Thad? Working? All work and no play make you a very dull boy."

"I like dull. I like simple. That's too much for you."

"It's not. Come on Thad." She pouted seductively wrapping her arms around his neck. "One night for good old times. We can celebrate all night for no reason at all. You'll enjoy every moment of it, I promise."

He moved her arms from around his neck. "I don't think that will be possible, Nicole. I am honored by the thought that you would consider me." Thaddeus stood to make his presence known that he was not pleased with her behavior. "I think it is time for me to go home."

Gathering his briefcase and laptop brief, he headed for the door. Even if his bedroom brought back too many memories, he would rather sit there and mope about Skye and the Case than to be in Nicole's presence any longer than he had too.

She disappointedly followed him out the offices to the elevator. "So I guess that means no?"

Thaddeus pushed the button to go down to the parking level where he was parked. "It's been no since Craig showed me his wedding invitation which I had no idea about. You took a perfectly good arrangement and turned it into a selfish affair. My trust in you is nil and I wouldn't reconsider if we were the last people on earth you were lying naked and I was horny as a rabbit. My hand would just become my best friend." He stepped off the elevator to go to his car. Before the doors closed in her face, he turned to her, raised a dark brow in a wickedly amusing way, to ask, "Did I make my no clear enough?"

She didn't have a chance to respond before the door closed on her and she was headed back upstairs to the lobby.

Getting home to the apartment, he showered and then laid down with a grim look on his face. Skye had made no attempt to get in touch with him yet he wanted to contact her, without being pushy. She wasn't playing hard to get. She was too innocent for games.

Innocent was a strong word. She just didn't seem like the deceptive type although he had thought the same of Nicole. It was amazing how he had the greatest sense about business, but when it came to women in his personal life, he had never chosen well. Even though he had told himself after Nicole he would give up women in his life, he found the most extraordinary woman in the most ordinary place. Maybe it was fate or destiny. It didn't matter, he wanted more than just one night from Skye Patterson. He wanted . . . forever.

Why shouldn't he want any less? He was almost thirty, successful and single. It shouldn't be this way, yet it was, but he didn't want to be unhappy and he didn't want a woman who wanted him for just his success. He wanted a woman for her mind and what she did to his. Skye was this woman.

Curiosity was also driving him to find out how she could be like his mystery woman. Would he ever know? It was killing him to know the identity of "the case", which he had begun to call the mystery woman. This was becoming a frustrating matter in his life; which woman he wanted. It was impossible to be in love with two women. He concluded the matter by lusting "the case" and love Skye. He just wished it were the same woman, but that would be in his dreams!

Chapter 9

"So you'll be there, right?"

Skye was a bit hesitant. "I guess. Do you want me to bring you anything?"

Trisha thought about it a second, then declined. "No, you don't. My mother will have everything."

"I appreciate you inviting me."

"It's no problem. I appreciate you accepting."

Skye replaced the receiver thoughtfully. Dinner at Trisha's mother home would be tonight. Going down to the basement again, she picked up the red gown. She hadn't been down there for five days. Skye had purposely kept herself busy so she wouldn't have to think about the nightgown. Quickly she put the gown in the washing machine along with other delicate clothes.

Before going back to work, she laid out a nice red cotton dress with black shoes and a matching jacket. Rolling her hair up tightly, she mailed some more reports in that she had not done earlier, and then started typing again. It was going to be another long weekend for her, but she wanted a social life and Trisha was only being nice. Trisha told Skye that there was a birthday dinner party for a friend of the family, and it was perfectly fine if she attended. More people meant a bigger party and it would give Skye a chance to get out which she hardly ever did.

At six she finished her shower and began to dress. Getting into her Escort she wondered if she should take a birthday card. Going to the nearest *Hallmark* store, she found a simple, but funny card and also bought two movie passes. It wasn't anything big, but she thought it would be nice instead of just crashing a party even if the daughter had invited her.

"I must be crazy," she told herself getting back in the car again. Arriving on the eastside of Detroit, Trisha came out the house and hugged her tightly. "Did you have a problem getting here?"

"No, your directions were pretty good. Has the festivities started?"

"The birthday boy isn't due here until late. Please come in, I want you to meet my family."

Which was what passed the time so quickly. She found Trisha's family to be quite engaging and when it was known she was Sybil Howard, many women were intrigued and wanted to know when she'd be doing a book signing. One of Trisha's sisters, Ella worked at a bookstore and insisted for Skye to come out and do a book reading at least. She would be surprised at how many fans she really did have in Detroit.

Skye gave Ella her card and told her to call her with more information. Although she wrote extensively she had only done most of her book signing in Ohio and Illinois. She had also gone to several book fairs out the state and even book fairs in Canada and Europe, but she never thought of a market in Michigan.

"Detroiters read, we just don't like to admit it," Ella teased. "I can't keep your recent book on the shelf. It would be so profitable for you to come in and do a book reading. Do you have one in works too?"

"I always have one in work. Usually several, but I try to concentrate on one at a time, but it's difficult with so much running through my mind and life."

Trisha cut in, "I must admit that I enjoy your plots as well as your love scenes. You have a way to make me rush past the love scenes to get the mystery out the way, then go back slowly and enjoy the love scenes even more."

"I know I just cried when Trevor in *Daze in Summer* found his father after all those years," Trisha's mother said. "Trish has me reading your books like crazy."

Trisha disappeared from the crowd of women, but returned immediately. "I must steal her away. Alan just came." Trisha guided her through the old colonel house out to the back door on the large wooden deck. Trisha's dad was over the Grill with a cute red apron on that read, "Kiss the Cook." He was sweating, yet there was an ethereal look upon his face that made him look at peace with himself. Anyone could plainly see this man took some sort of pleasure out of being the cook.

A tall man about six feet tall with sharp features, turned towards them. Skye haltered a bit. His beady black eyes seemed familiar, but she couldn't remember where. Trisha nudged her forward.

"Skye, I'd like you to meet my fiancé, Trevor-Alan Coleman."

He stretched out his hand. "Nice to meet you. Trisha speaks highly of you."

"Thank you," she said still a bit dazed by the man. His shake was firm and quick as if the more she touched him the more she would find out about him. Then out of nowhere, there was an echo in her head, "*Make the bad man go away.*" A shiver passed through her body and the beady black eyes that stared at her squinted hard.

Backing away, she turned about. "I have to go to the bathroom," she muttered and moved quickly in the house.

Trisha frowned and looked up at Alan who looked just as baffled as her. He had an "I-told-you-so" expression in his eyes, which she tried to avoid.

Running up the stairs, she found the bathroom close to the top. Splashing cold water on her face, her body fought control of the panic attack gripping at her being. She purposely didn't bring any medicine so she would not get disoriented. She had stopped taking them, but the panic attack was gripping her hard, enfolding her body like an envelope. Burying her face in the towel, she fought mentally to get control.

Suddenly strong warm arms encircled her body. Initially, she tightened up then relaxed feeling light as a feather and warm all over. A comforting deep voice whispered in her ear.

Skye immediately realized she still as Trisha mom's house and not alone. Looking up she gasped, tightening up again. How had he gotten here? Why the heck was he holding her? Pushing away, she was still disoriented.

"I-I'm sorry." she apologized.

Thaddeus straightened his jacket a little. "No need. You were shaking and crying. I didn't know what else to do."

"I was?" she asked going back over to the mirror after neatly replacing the towel. She looked plain again. The lipstick she had on previously was gone. Reaching in her purse, she pulled out some more. Out the corner of her eye she was watching him watch her. He leaned against the door while she applied more lipstick.

"Thank you." She put the lipstick back in her purse. "I don't know what was wrong with me?" She forced a smile to assure him and herself that everything was fine.

"You seem to be out of it. Is everything really okay, Ms Patterson?" He was genuinely concerned stepping close to her.

She took a step back, unsure what she would do with him so close. "Fine, Mr. Newman. I am fine. Thank you again. I didn't realize I had caused alarm."

"You walked right by me downstairs?"

"I did?" she asked surprised. "I didn't see you." This was the absolute truth.

"Trisha asked me to come and check on you."

"Like I said, I'm fine." She turned away deliberately so she wouldn't face him.

He conceded. "Then I'll see you downstairs."

When he left she breathed a sigh of relief leaning against the sink in embarrassment. Why did he make her feel so uptight yet relaxed at the same time? Should she feel this way? Why was it so hard to maintain her equilibrium when he was around?

* * *

Thaddeus stopped at the top of the stairs. Why did he feel like an ass whenever he thought he was doing something good for her? Why was he persistent in seeing her when he knew she had no interest in him? She barely looked at him.

Trisha saw him come down stairs not looking pleased. The grim expression on his face made him so unapproachable. He was the birthday boy and this was his party, yet he was choosing to spend this day in a depressed fashion.

Moving up to him, she simply asked if Skye was all right.

He nodded then moved past her to greet her mother and father. Trisha went upstairs to see Skye putting on her coat.

"Are you leaving?"

"Yes," Skye said simply that brook no argument from Trisha.

"But the honored person, just arrived."

"That honored person happens to be a man I feel uncomfortable around and I don't see why I should spend another moment here. You tricked me Trisha and I trusted you like an idiot." Moving past Trisha she headed for the stairs. Trisha caught up with her begging her to slow down.

"Just stay until after dinner and then leave. My parents won't understand your leaving and my mother is so excited to have you. She thinks of herself as your biggest fan."

Skye knew she was only putting icing on a dry cake, and nothing would get better for her in this present situation she found herself mentally in. Things were not going to change about her new feeling for Thaddeus. Instead, being around him her feeling were destine to get stronger and she would not be able to control them anymore as she had been in the past. He would never feel for her as she felt for him. Only in her dreams.

Yet, Sky enjoyed Trisha's family. The family had a bond, which she wished she had grown up with. Especially Trisha's dad who Skye could tell adored his daughter to pieces. She knew now why Trisha was so wonderful to be around, although she sensed some tension between Alan and Trisha's father, but she couldn't explain the feelings between them. Skye had a feeling Alan was not welcomed in this house.

Still she could not enjoy this time with Thaddeus proximity. With a deflated sigh, she said, "Trish, I can't. As much as I find him interesting right now, I don't think I can enjoy myself being so nervous around him. I'd act like a ninny."

Trisha felt Skye deserved a good time and on the other hand felt warmly about Thaddeus too. He was her boss, yet he felt like a brother. She had been with him from almost the beginning, and she wanted him to be happy as well. Thaddeus had worked extremely hard to get where he was today and now that he was where he wanted to be on his business side, Trisha felt it was time to get what he wanted on a personal side and if Skye was what he wanted, Trisha would help him get her. Yet, Skye had also become a good friend and upsetting her was not Trisha's goal. "Fine, but please let me have Alan walk you to your car." Before Skye could protest, she said, "I insist unless you want me to get Mr. Newman."

Just wanting to get out of there without letting Trisha know how really upset she was with everything, Skye conceded. "That will be fine. I'll be at the front door with my coat."

Trisha gave her a hug and went downstairs to find Alan. Before getting her coat, Skye washed her face again, and then she noticed she needed to refresh her lipstick. She had set her small purse down on the bed where all the coats were in the room across from the bathroom. Going in there without turning on the light, she heard someone stop at the doorway and begin to make a cell phone call. Thinking this was Thaddeus who had come back up again because she saw the person check the bathroom, she stayed in the darkened room unnoticed waiting for him to go away. He didn't. The dark figure began to speak on the cell phone.

"It's Alan . . . Yes I have it. I left the samples in my car, Dr. Himes."

The name certainly piqued her attention. She took a chance and moved closer to the doorway. Leaning near a dresser, she was covered just in case he decided to come in the room she could duck down.

"The list is in my coat. I will be there after I finish the business I am at now. Let my father know she doesn't recognize me. His fear was useless."

Skye frowned at this wondering what he was speaking about.

She remembered what coat he was wearing. It was a long leather jacket that laid right near hers.

"I said I would be there soon. You've been waiting all year for this information, a couple of hours is not going to kill you." He cut the phone off, cursed to himself, and then went downstairs.

She went to the bed and started searching in the pockets of his coat. In the inside coat pocket her fingers touched some paper. Pulling it out, she began to read the dot matrix print out. There were names of women. She wondered why Dr. Himes would need this copy. Skye also noted that at the top of the paper read Family Independence Agency High Thyroid Cases. Beside the women's numbers were case numbers. Suddenly, it dawned on her what this contained.

These women were going to become candidates in Dr. Himes' Depro Second Phaze Study. Of course this was all an assumption. He planned to administer the drug to all these women. Why did she have a feeling none of these women would know they were being tested on?

Remembering Trisha's mother telling her that she ran a home business and her office was upstairs in the attic, Skye made her way up the attic stairs. Her luck kept going as she saw a copier and it was already on. Quickly she made a copy of the paper and went back in the coatroom.

Unfortunately her luck ran out, because just as she entered the room, Alan and Trisha came in speaking heatedly to each other.

"Why do you have to go now?" she complained. "You promised to speak with Daddy tonight, Trevor-" they both stopped seeing Skye in the room as he turned on the light.

"Thank you," Skye said relieved. "I was wondering why I couldn't find my things." She hid both hands behind her remembering his papers were in her right hand. "It is rather late. Way past my bedtime."

Alan looked at his watched. "It's eight o'clock."

Skye faked a yawn. "Whew! That late?"

Alan ignored her turning to Trisha. "Trish, I have things to do," he said irritated by her constant complaining. He moved by Skye and picked up his coat.

Skye dropped his paper as soon as he lifted the coat from the bed, then immediately reached down and picked it up, stuffing her copy in her coat quickly while picking up the dropped copy at the same time. "You dropped this, Alan," she said handing the paper to him.

He almost gasped, but stopped himself. Meeting her eyes, those beady black eyes peered her over distrustfully.

Skye picked up her purse off the bed and moved to the door by Trisha trying not to look guilty. "Is Alan going to walk me to my car while he is going out?" she asked innocently.

"That would be no problem," Alan agreed.

Skye hugged Trisha. "Thank you for not convincing me to stay. I don't think my nerves could take it."

"You're quite welcome. Your presence was certainly appreciated. Aunt Vera will have something to speak about for years to come at all the upcoming family gatherings."

Skye laughed a throaty pleased laugh genuinely pleased her presence had brought some happiness to someone.

"Goodnight." They hugged knowing they speak soon on a later date.

Skye went down to the living room, giving the couple some privacy, but she could still partially hear what they said, because they didn't close the door to the room.

". . . invite her here? You go through all the trouble with me to make sure. . . . Now you do what you want to do anyway. You'd better stop it Trisha. If my father knew what you were doing. . . ."

"I know and I will. You will call later?" She asked hopefully.

Aunt Vera stepped up to Skye suddenly. "You're leaving?"

"Unfortunately I am." She acknowledged the older woman knowing she could not listen to them anymore. "I loved the company, but I have so much to do. Thank you so much for having me."

"Thank you for coming. We are all so glad to have you."

Skye patted her pocket to make sure the copied paper was deep in there and secure.

Alan came down the stairs right after with Trisha behind him who looked ready to protest. She watched as Alan escorted Skye out.

Skye feeling uncomfortable pulled away from his gentle gripped as they went down the stairs. "You work on your own, Alan?" she asked when they got to her car.

He seemed surprised she would be interested in something he did. "N-No," he stuttered quickly off beat. "You could say that I handle my father's international interest."

"You must lead quite an interesting life." She backed to the car door unlocked it then backed into the car. "Good night."

He thought her behavior quite odd, but said nothing to the fact. He wanted to hurry and get this list to the doctors. He was hoping Skye didn't see any similarities between him and his father. "Goodnight."

Trisha walked up to Thaddeus who stood at the window watching the black Escort disappear in the night.

"Did you cancel my flight to Florida tomorrow night?" he asked knowing she was standing behind him.

"Yes, but I did want to ask you why? You've always gone the two days prior to see Mr. Blair, before your scheduled appointment with him every year."

"Unfortunately this one falls on a Saturday and I have another appointment tomorrow night."

"With whom, if I may be so bold to ask?"

He faced her. "None of your business if I may be so bold to answer."

Her father handed him his coat and thanked him for coming then left them to speak alone again. "It's a young woman if you must know."

"A woman? I thought your interest in Ms Patterson, was serious."

"It is. I am man hear me roar. I have needs like any other man."

She nodded rather shocked. "Did you want me to do anything?"

"If you could have some red wine delivered to my apartment

tomorrow and scented candles again. I had a hell of a time picking some out and I don't think I did a good job." He passed her a non-duplicable key. "Leave this key on my bedside table please. I'm trying to create a mood if you get my drift."

She nodded. "I do. You won't mind if I help you out a bit?"

He raised a dark brow. "How?"

"Trust me. I am woman, hear me roar," she said throwing his words back at him. This lightened his mood a good deal.

At that point they were interrupted again, as her mother brought over a large plate of food all wrapped up for him. Walking to the door with Thaddeus, Trisha's mom let him know if he was always invited and she hoped he had a happy birthday. Trisha looked down at the key and smiled devilishly. He would tomorrow night all right.

Chapter 10

When he arrived at his apartment the next night after spending all morning at a videoconference downtown with Mr. Thomas Blair, he was rather shocked to see the place glowing with candles in the front room.

He was up since six that morning where he met Craig at a coffee shop in Highland Park to discuss the blood test they took from his mystery woman last week.

"She's got a clean bill of health according to the doctor. Fingerprints show she doesn't have a record."

Thaddeus cut him off. "Who is she?" he demanded to know.

Craig held the folder close to his chest. "Sergeant Nolan made me swear not to reveal her identity nor any of the other girls. The less you know about her the easy it will be to tear yourself away from this case."

"Tear myself away? You act as if I'm obsessed about her."

Craig leaned into the table to Thaddeus. "If you weren't, you wouldn't be so damned demanding."

Thaddeus forced himself to relax and take control of his stamina. "You've never listened to your sergeant before this. Why is it so critical that her identity be hidden from me?"

"Look Thad. When this is all over you're never going to see her again. I thought you could stay apart from the whole situation and use it to your advantage. What is happening is all it—*now,* nothing else. There won't be any memory of you in her life according the Dr. Powers and if there is it won't be enough for her to remember clearly. There's not going to be any riding into the sunset of knight in shining armor to rescue her or everyone will live happily ever after. You can't force or browbeat me in any kind of way to get me to reveal anything about this young lady because I know you and how you get obsessive about things although I thought a woman would be the last thing you'd get obsessive about. If you feel it's that important then you can step out now." Craig regretted the words as soon as they left this mouth, and prayed Thaddeus wouldn't pull his card again.

Thaddeus sat back thinking. Craig was right. This was the now and to pull out would be ridiculous, immature, and could jeopardize lives. "Fine. No identities need to be told—for now." He left it open intentionally to put Craig on the edge. He knew he was being ridiculous, but he had to be difficult some way since he couldn't pull Craig's card.

"Aside from all of it, you're doing an excellent job. Fats has put his guard down, but I don't want to push it. Do you have the form we asked your doctor to fill out?"

"Yes, but why did I have to have him fill it out."

"Mainly for peace of mind, in case you . . . slip up."

"What? I don't slip up."

"For mistakes, temptations, that sort of thing."

He angrily handed the form to Craig. "This is really starting to get on my nerves, Craig."

"Didn't seem that way last week," Craig teased ignoring the vicious glare he received for that remark and whooped with laughter loudly drawing a little attention to them. No one else would dare rile him so dangerously, but Craig had known him for so long, it was normal for him to do so.

"Remind me to beat your ass when I'm not killing mad at you. If I do it now I might cause death and I won't have the pleasure of seeing you suffer for the rest of your miserable life."

Craig chuckled some more. "Get on down the road, Bro."

That had been the gist of conversation, but it had pretty much been on Thaddeus' mind all day. His mystery woman would be here soon and it pleased him to know he could do whatever he wanted. Anything!

It wasn't until now that he realized this. Damn! Knowing he could make hard passionate love to her aroused him even more.

'Are you crazy?!' his conscious raged. Thaddeus was past crazy. He was horny and he wanted his mystery woman to quench his lust.

The entire apartment was scented with lavender a rather exotic smell that he enjoyed. Trisha wrote a Post-it-Note ® hanging on his bedroom door.

Mr. Newman, Only enter this room with the intentions of coming out and spending the night with your mystery woman on the couch. You need a change of environment to relax you. Try it and I swear it will be a night you will never forget. See you in the morning, Trisha

He wondered if Trisha knew something he didn't. Entering the bedroom, he saw the package on the bed. Opening it, another note from Trisha was there above the tissue wrapping.

Put it on and get out of here!

Pulling the tissue wrap off, there was a black silk robe, matching boxers, and some nice black bedroom shoes. He showered quickly and then stared at the outfit for a long while, before he gave in and put it on. For whatever reason, he succumbed to Trisha's orders. For some strange reason the young woman had been on his mind all week. Seductive and enticing, he wondered why had he thought about her with as much thought as he'd thought about Skye. Her face didn't even matter, but what she made him feel did. Tonight he decided he would go ahead and please her. After dressing, he went to the kitchen to prepare the glasses of wine. Trisha had put a bottle in the refrigerator to chill.

Marking the sleeping potion glass with a scratch, he went into the living room. Stopping short in his track was the young lady with her back to him putting a nice classical piece on. He placed the glasses down on the coffee table and joined her by the stereo. She took one hand and placed his palm on her breast, and then she took the other hand and placed it on her crotch. He could feel his manhood rise in his next quickening breath. He closed his eyes and allowed her body to caress against his. He could feel her nipple tight in his palm until it was a hard nub.

"Why did you come back?" he asked

"I wanted to be with you."

"Who sent you?"

She turned and tucked her face in the crook of his neck. He could smell her essence of lavender. "You should know all this."

"Where did you come from?" It was a silly questioned and she chuckled sensuously in response.

"Where every one else comes from. Will we make love tonight or will you just hold me again? I want you so much more now."

In one swoop he picked her up and carried her to the couch. Laying her down on the couch, their lips melted together perfectly. His whole body seem to tense then relax as her warm tongue pushed against his lips. He parted his own to welcome the moist oral muscle in. She deepened the kiss wrapping her arms around his neck and pulling him closer. He could feel her body shudder in his arms. Her wantonness for him stirred him to great heights of passion. The more she was pleased the more it urged him on to please her even more.

He pushed the robe off her shoulders pulling the straps down from her gown in this same movement. Reluctantly, his lips departed from hers. She whimpered in protest, and then moaned in pleasure as he found the aroused firm dark brown nipple and suckled the tempting flesh deeply.

She gasped as her fingers tightened in his hair. Her head went back as her body leaned into his mouth. He smiled when he heard her whine as his lips moved over to her other nipple. Her sexual frustration was clearly evident as her hips rubbed against his thick strapping thigh.

Pushing the gown past her knees in one fluid movement was easy. Her passion aroused him to an unbelievable level of unguided ardor. His lips followed his hands downward, pressing hot wet kisses against her skin. He didn't know what he was doing or even want to think about making sense. All he knew was he wanted to give her pleasure. He wanted to know that her wantonness was because of what he did to her. It felt wonderful to know whatever he did to her or touch of her, made her crave more of him.

Gently nudging her body prone, his mouth descended to the soft brown thatch of hair. The tip of his tongue made a trail from her belly to the forest of thick hair, until wetness met his own. Her hips lounged off the couch. Thaddeus took this opportunity to skillfully wrap his arms around her thighs and clamp his hands around her hips to control her powerful waist. Her back was fully arched as his mouth began to draw the essence from her body. She tried to twist, but he was tortuous in his pleasure giving until she could only whimper her protest. Soon her whimpers turned to begging as his tongue assaulted her repeatedly until he too could feel pleasure racking every nerve in her body.

She shook uncontrollably as every nerve peaked simultaneously taking her high above the heavens, wrapping her in glorious sensations, then enveloped her body with the most pure form of pleasure a man could give a woman. She felt loved through every inch of her body and no one could tell her this experience had not happened to her.

He knew the orgasm had blown her mind and helped her body come down slowly from the pinnacle he had taken her too. He made another trail of kisses until his mouth was above hers.

The candles were almost out, yet he could make out her eyes sparkling darkly up at him and for a moment he thought he was looking at Skye. He told himself he was crazy as she cupped his face in her palms and brought him down to her lips. He kissed her with all the force of passion he felt right now, because he could almost imagine this was Skye. He could almost imagine Skye being here with him, feeling the intensity. He wanted so much for this to be Skye, but he knew it would never be, not until she could even like him. Hell, maybe even longer.

Lord what had he done? He'd used a woman to replace another. Craig was right. It wasn't fair to her and he was a bastard to put this woman who had no idea what she was doing through this.

Moving away from her feeling very guilty, he grabbed the unscratched glass and gulped it down. She watched him. He was deeply troubled at this point, but she didn't know how to take his troubles away.

Standing up, he went to the kitchen to pour himself another glass. If he really thought about it, he hadn't done anything wrong.

Giving her pleasure couldn't possibly destroy her sense of realism or give her nightmares. Making love to her would not confuse her either. He *needed* to make love to her just because of the fact in his mind he thought she looked like Skye sometimes. Skye was all he really saw and thought about. Pretending she was Skye made this all the more bearable.

Filling the glass up, he went back into the living room determined to make love to her. She was still lying on the couch, her arms slightly covering her face and one leg down on the floor. Her eyes were closed and she was breathing deeply.

He looked at the coffee table to see some of the scratched glass contents were lowered and there was a drop of liquid on the corner of her mouth. Sighing in pure disappointment, he sat at the edge of the couch facing her. In the dim light she really did favor Skye, but the make up and hair through him off. He never saw Skye with her hair down so he couldn't really say how she looked to differ from this woman. Skye's hair was always in a neat tight bun and seemed darker. Not this honey colored curly hair the young woman had.

Sipping his glass slowly, his eyes began to wander down her body, visually caressing the handful size breast with the dark nipples, and the flat belly with a birthmark that looked like a hammer right below her rib cage. Her navel was small and he could tell she had never born a child because of the size of the slim hips she possessed and unmarked belly. He was drawn to touch the soft thatch again and in her sleep she groaned, then rolled over to her side. With her face hidden in the crook of her elbow, he found himself clearly aroused just knowing this could be Skye. Her voluptuous posterior rounded quite nicely flowing into the curve of her thigh.

He leaned back becoming comfortable in his half way prone position. Soon his eyelids became heavy. He wanted to try to wait until the potion wore off, so he could speak to her again, but sleep enveloped him quickly.

Chapter 11

Thaddeus awakened to a light tapping on the front door. He looked at the couch in front of him to see no one lying there. There was nothing to really say there had been anyone over except for the lipstick on the second glass and the long strands of honey brown hair.

Getting up slowly, stretching his back, he tightened the robe closed as he looked out the peephole. Opening the door, he nodded only a good morning at Trisha who stood just smiling up at him.

"Your plane leaves at ten."

"What time is it?"

"Eight. Have you even packed?"

"Some." He nodded over to the suitcases near the front door. "You need to finish packing my suits only."

"Well, I think I can manage that. Would you like some coffee?"

He nodded heading to the bedroom and closing the door.

Trisha went to the kitchen and quietly fixed some coffee listening to his every move. Soon she heard him in the shower and quickly began to look through the cabinets, but found nothing, which she thought would be there. He was quick with the shower and when he was done, she waited until he came out dressed in khaki's and a nice shirt. He was too handsome and she wondered what a man like him was doing single. Why was he so elusive?

"Does Ms Patterson still type for us?"

"Reluctantly yes. Do you want me to keep her?"

"Of course." He handed her some micro cassettes. "These are from my videoconference. I want you to send Terrance over to Ms Patterson's home and make sure she is set up on PCAnywhere as soon as possible. When you're out of town, I can depend on her to get the work I need done in the city. Pay her whatever you have to."

"Yes Mr. Newman." She went to the phone to call the usual courier service the company always used to deliver the tapes and instructions over to Skye's house. As he spoke more instructions, she shorthanded them knowing Skye would be able to understand.

"When will you be leaving?" he asked.

"Nine tonight. I will meet you for breakfast at eight in the morning in the hotel's lobby."

"Make it six. I have some business at seven-thirty and I am looking forward to spending the rest with Thomas."

She could tell he was eager to see him. Thomas Blair was a good friend of Thaddeus since college. It was Thomas who had front the money for Thaddeus to start Newman Enterprises. It was also Thomas who had gotten Thaddeus to even consider running a business on his own when Thaddeus was working for others and making them successful. Thomas gained his money from his grandfather who was a stockbroker and knew investments like the back of his hand. Thomas was just as good and had created his own fortune, but none of this seemed to please the man.

"I'm going to make some stops then I'll be going to the airport. Could you make sure my suits are at the hotel by tomorrow morning? I trust your opinion, and I will see you at six." He grabbed a jacket out of the front closet, took his suitcase and left. He knew the sleeping serum hid in a secret compartment in the back of the cabinet in the kitchen was safe from anyone knowing. Even he had a hard time remembering which one was the secret place, but he knew he could not trust anyone with what he was doing. In addition to this, he didn't want to entrust Trisha with the case information. As close as he felt to her, he knew her fiancé would not like her keeping secrets from him.

He knew that Trisha's father didn't trust Alan, and the young man seemed leery of Thaddeus. Thaddeus knew this was probably because Trisha had to travel with him a lot, but he really saw Trisha in a light almost like a sister. Even less. It was almost like a sister's friend who he had no intention to gain any more on their relationship. They kept it strictly platonic, just business.

After Trisha finished packing his things, she left the suits and the tapes at the front desk of the Riverfront apartments for the courier service. After that she went home to finish packing her clothes and say goodbye to Alan who promised to come by before she left.

Her pager went off just as she finished packing. Going to the phone, she called the number back. "Hello Skye, you called me?"

"Yes, I know you told me yesterday you'd be out of town for two days, but I just wanted to let you know, I received the tapes and instructions. I will start on them immediately."

"Thanks. Terrance is waiting on your call and since you are familiar with the software, I don't think you'll have a problem with it."

"I could just install it myself and call Terrance with any technical questions."

"That would be fine. You can leave messages on my voicemail. I will check it every two hours."

"I think I will be fine. Call me if you need anything here before you get back."

They spoke more, but Trisha heard no worried fluctuation in her voice. She was appeased with what she heard and let Skye go after a while.

*   *   *

Hanging up the receiver, Skye breathe a sigh of relief. She figured she had played that off rather smoothly. Looking down at the package the courier had just delivered knowing fully well what it was. Her body shook again. Quickly she sat down in the nearest chair to regain her composure. Just thinking about what she dreamed made nerve-racking spasms overcome her. She had placed three voicemails to Dr. Carter's service and didn't know what else to do.

"You've got mail!" her computer said excitedly.

Looking at the computer screen, a little mailbox flashed, then went still.

She went to the desk and slowly sat down in the chair in front of the monitor. Wiggling the mouse, the screen flashed two messages. Double clicking, the first message quickly opened from a Dr. Robert Hardwick in Southfield, Michigan.

In response to your question, I haven't heard of this drug since the early testing of it in 1993 in France when they were trying to increase sexual emotions in woman because of the decrease sexual intensity Depro-Vera produces. I don't know a lot about it, but I do know that you can have a great amount of hallucinations, dreaming and auditory fantasies. There would be no way to get the drug out of your system, but I would prescribe Thorazime to take the effects of the hallucinations away, but it will make you sleepy. Speak to the doctor who prescribe the drug, and if you can't do that, you may contact my offices. My number is below the automated signature in the email.

Call me anytime.

After printing off the email, she double clicked to bring up the next one.

Hello Skye,

I do apologize for taking so long to answer your calls or your emails. Our small town has been so busy with many fall activities. You know how this time of year is here. You use to help coordinate most of the events. Well it's not the same without you or your smile. Nurse Stephanie says hello and she misses you as well as many of your other associates. Don't have time in the big city to call them, huh? Well I know this is your first experience by yourself and you're just settling in.

Now back to business. That drug you specified as 'sic' was very hard to look up. No ones heard about it or don't want to speak about. I finally found some intern who said he worked in Dr. Carter's office in Detroit for about six months before he was conveniently fired for 'being too nosey.' He said the drug is a form of GHB mixed with Depro-Vera to control the subconscious. He knew Dr. Carter was trying to get it approved by the government, but they didn't feel that this should be used in women as a form of sexual stimulant with a birth control twist. He was trying to compete with the Viagra market for women, but the government disapproved too much of the drug due to it's high GHB content. If you can obtain a sample, but you don't feel comfortable sending it through the mail there is a contact in a medical West Bloomfield laboratory that can assist you.

If you need anything else that I can help you with let me know and I will make sure it is just between you and I. Take care and I do hope you are well.
Dr. Welch

Hearing from Dr. Welch perked her up a bit, but knowing the drug was not good and in her system did not make her feel any better. Control her subconscious? Why would Dr. Himes want to control her subconscious? When she tried to think about what he could be doing to her while she was in this state made her stomach fly into a million butterflies.

What would happen when she went into the state again? When would she go into this state again? Sleeping? Awake? When did it happen?

Sitting on the loveseat in her home office, she tried to remember the dreams that she had been having lately. It was difficult to remember, but she was positive she had no control over these dreams and these dreams had something to do with the drug in her body.

Lying down, she made herself relax and remember. Her stomach felt full of butterflies trying to get out.

". . . be mine," a voice whispered . . . candlelight . . . black silk boxers . . . the smell of lavender . . . kissing—nice sensual kissing . . . a scar below the collarbone . . . she licked it.

Sitting up opening her eyes, she tried to scontrol her vapid breathing. Going back to her computer she picked up a notepad and pencil and drew the oval with a beveled line coming from the center out past the edge of the oval. In her memory, the oval was crooked and there was a light vertical line-marking running from each side of the oval.

Why could she remember this mark so well? Why couldn't she see the face of this mystery man, yet she felt she knew him, knew of him?

Thaddeus. Why did it seem to fit so nicely?

'Because that is what you want, silly and you *know* it could never be true,' she told herself.

'This is not a dream,' she tried to convince herself, but turned around and asked, 'What is it then?'

That was the million-dollar question. Who was it?

'Torturing yourself isn't doing anything for your pocket book, Skye.' She plopped down at the computer and put the tape on. As she began typing the note, the voice seemed to drone in her head.

Her fingers lifted off the keyboard and she read what she had just typed in the past five minutes.

Be mine.

Where did you come from?

Be mine.

Why did you come back?

Who sent you?

Why would her mystery man ask her these questions of this sort, when it should be her asking these questions? Furthermore, why the heck was she typing this and not what was on the tape.

Rewinding the tape to the beginning she forced herself to concentrate on Thaddeus' dictation. It was a letter to a Heaven Wineguard of Chicago.

"Ms. Wineguard, It has come to my attention that you were part of the adoption process of a female child born December 9. 1977. To my understanding you were the one that was in charge of sealing the record to anyone who wanted to inquire about the adoption process. It is also my understanding that five years after the adoption was done, it was ruled an illegal adoption due to the fact Judge Henry Prophet received information that both parents had not signed a form giving their release to the child. The father's signature was forged. Under orders from Judge Prophet, he has given me permission to secure these records so that

I may use my own means to find the female birth child of Thomas Blair. Typist please signature myself and cc: Thomas Blair, Judge Henry Prophet and Lethal R. Heart of Lethal Security and Investigation Services, thank you. "

She did as she was told and immediately e-mailed the letter to his address, cc-ing Trisha as well.

The other letters were not as interesting as the first, but she quickly typed them and got them out the way before she stopped working for the day and decided to take a long hot bath. The whole weekend had been rather stressful for her. Maybe she should just drop the entire Newman account. It would make her life simple again like in the beginning before involving herself with this whole matter. So what the money was good, peace of mind outweighed everything and Thaddeus Newman did not give her peace of mind.

Yet, Sheila and Margaret were definitely enjoying the different work and the bonuses she had given for their excellent turn-around times and professional typing was gratefully appreciated. Skye hardly needed to type unless there was an overload or unless she just wanted to. She enjoyed that aspect of her home business the most.

Lying in bed she looked at the pillow beside her. Empty. It would always be empty if she didn't get her butt out the house and meet more interesting people. She would call up that friend Gladys in Davenport had told her to look up when she got here. It wouldn't be so bad. This whole dreaming thing could all be from the seclusion she accepted since she had been to Detroit.

Chapter 12

Thomas closed the curtain longingly and turned toward Thaddeus who had been like a son to him. "She would have been twenty-three today, Thad."

Thaddeus was use to the older man drifting off on days that should have been. Thomas was going on fifty-two and with the knowledge of never having an offspring since his stroke eight years ago, he had been on a desperate search to find a child that was given up for adoption. His mother put an injunction against the adoption process because it was her only grandchild and the baby girl was given to a foster home until a decision could be made. The judge making the decision had died, and a year passed before the next date was set for a new trial. During that time, Thomas mother died and no one went up to support the family. Thomas had involved himself in investments outside of the country and the last thing on his mind was a bastard in Chicago. The child was left in foster care then lost in the system. Last thing they were able to pull up was that the child had run away from the last foster home. No other news had come to them about her.

He blamed himself for all of it. Thomas could not imagine what this girl must feel for her parents about now. Many told him to give up, but he kept hope that she would be alive and willing to forgive a man who was stupid, young and had not realized the power of carrying on his blood line until it was too late.

"Don't beat yourself up anymore, Thomas. If she's out there Heart will find her. He said he received positive leads in Sante Fe, Dallas and Toronto. He plans to check them all out with a fine tooth comb and get back to us."

"I know this." Thomas sat across from Thaddeus noticing the young man had not touched his vodka and coke Thomas had made when Thaddeus walked in. "You still on that trip?"

Thaddeus patted his chest. "I will continue to be on this trip as long as I have this scar to remind me about the errors of drinking." He had been so consumed with alcohol it had made him blind to see how devious Nicole really was.

"Suit yourself." He picked up the drink and took a swallow. "Now who's beating themselves up? I say go whoop her ass for getting you to do it."

"Right about now, I really don't want to think of Nicole. I plan to stay far away from her and her kind."

"I noticed you've been staying out of the social circle."

"Trying my best. Mother invited me to Europe this summer, but I plan to decline."

"Why is that? You've always jumped at chances to spend time with your mother."

"I have business in Detroit." He smirked secretly.

"Fash, you can do business anywhere . . . why the hell are you smirking like that?" He then chuckled. "I guess you can't do that everywhere if it's only in Detroit."

Thaddeus flushed. "Quite true, but not just that. I've met a quite interesting woman who I find enjoyable to speak with. She's not like others. Pure pleasant."

"Odd. Never thought I would hear you speak of females as pure pleasant. She must be ugly."

"No Cleopatra, but far from breaking mirrors with a little help."

"A little help?"

"With the right incentive."

"That must be a treat. Female friends are hard to come by with a status like us, Thaddeus. If she's a gem, keep her."

"I plan to." He stood up. "I'd like to shower before dinner."

"Please do. Your room is always ready."

Thaddeus went up the stairs of the large colonial home.

This house had been in Thomas' family since after the Civil War. Thomas loved the house, but his business took him all over the world so he hardly enjoyed it, except on his birthday weekend, which all his closest friends gathered for a grand celebration on the weekend near his birthday, coming next weekend. The weekend prior to his birthday was time spent with Thaddeus for his daughter's birthday and people who showed up early. No one questioned why he celebrated a birthday for a daughter he had never known. He was wealthy and allowed to have his quirks.

Thaddeus had spoke to Fats and informed him he wouldn't be needing the services to the mystery woman next weekend, but to keep her to himself, he would still have to pay for that time slot. He knew this was fine with Craig, and if it wasn't he would pay for it from his own pocket.

Even now as he undressed to get more comfortable, he found that he missed her presence. Disturbing his thoughts was his pager going off. Looking at the screen he read, "8 New E-mails." Hooking his laptop, he downloaded them and realized they were from Skye. He replied to her last one, "Thank you for your prompt services. I hope they weren't too tiresome to transcribe."

Sending the e-mail he wondered if she would reply back with friendliness or just ignore another chance to talk to him.

Before he went to bed that night, he did check his e-mail one more time. Skye had written him back.

"Compared to the foreign doctors I usually get from my other accounts, I go through yours like a paddle in the water. Although, you shouldn't work so late. I can tell when you get tired because you begin to slur your words. I hope Florida treats you well."

He wrote back. "It's beautiful down here. Have you ever been to Florida?"

When he awoke the next morning he was quite surprised she had written back. "I haven't been two steps away from Davenport, Ohio since I was young except to come to Detroit. I miss the small city, but last night was my first night out in the city since I've been here and will honestly tell you, it was the best experience of city life I've yet to discover. You are so blessed you can travel so easily. I think on a traveling tip, I'd like to see Europe, but not by myself. What's to enjoy if you have no one to share the experience with. Oh dear, I've talked too much :)"

The e-mail ended there. Talked too much? No indeed. He'd quite enjoyed knowing that little bit about her.

Picking up the receiver, he dialed her number surprised he remembered it off the top of his head, yet he knew if he got it wrong he would end up calling Trisha, which he wanted to avoid.

"Hello," she answered.

"Good morning to you. Am I calling too early for you?"

There was a hesitant pause, then she said, "Oh no, I enjoy calls at seven am. I take it you are a morning person, Mr. Newman."

He chuckled at her sarcastic remark. "Quite. Were you up?"

"I was but not out of bed. I love waking up and just listening to the morning, meditating to myself, and being grateful at the opportunity to experience a new day. Have you ever done that?"

"Not of late. Usually I'm trying to get everything done by noon to enjoy the morning."

"You should try it once in a while. You might be surprised what you really can do to your whole self being." She sounded quite relaxed and comfortable. There was no doubt in his mind that she was still in bed.

"Listen to the morning? Don't you mean look at it?"

"No. Just lie in the bed and breathe deeply. Close your eyes and focus on the noises outside or in the house. You'd be surprised what a good state of mind you'll be in when you get to the middle part of the day. Especially if it's full of stress, which I'm sure yours is."

He considered it, but wondered what she would think if he asked her to join him one morning. Thaddeus decided not to mention this wicked thought. "I might try it. Tomorrow as a matter of fact and let you know if there was any difference."

"Good. Why don't you call me back then but not so early, so I can finish enjoying mine?"

Thaddeus hung up the phone in a fitful of laughter. She was truly a gem.

Thomas knocked quietly, and then opened the door. "Your mystery lady?"

"Far from it. She's the new woman I enjoy talking to and also one of my contract employees. I'll tell you again she's quite engaging. You'd certainly enjoy tangling minds with her, Thomas. I will invite her next year definitely."

"How do you know you will know her that long?"

"I intend to know Ms Patterson for a very long time."

"That sure of yourself? Fash, then, how 'bout Christmas if you find her that engaging."

"Yes, my company's Christmas party should be perfect for the event."

One of the housemaids came from downstairs and passed Thomas a note. Once he read it, then immediately frowned.

"What is it?" Thaddeus asked concerned.

Thomas crumpled the paper in agony sighing. "Agatha Washington died last week. Her lawyers would like me to come to her will reading this afternoon."

"This afternoon? What about the gala?"

"I should be back in time. Would you like to come with me? Moral support?"

Thaddeus shrugged. "I'd be in the way, but you know I'd stand by your side."

"Good. Let me get directions and time then we'll go from there."

"I'll call Trisha to reschedule some phone meetings and be right down."

Chapter 13

Entering the small offices of Newborn, Washington, and Fields, Thaddeus paid attention to the eyes that lit on him. He knew his size was impressive and he was far from being self conscious about it anymore.

Lester Newborn greeted them with a solemn smile. "It's a pleasure to finally meet you, Thomas. I've heard a lot about you, but to my surprise, Agatha never spoke of you. I know of you from other sources impressed with your investment skills."

"Agatha and I didn't part on good terms."

Thaddeus snorted knowing the truth. Thomas nudged him in the ribs. Lester told them to follow him. While doing this, Thaddeus whispered in Thomas ear. "I thought she was a dancer."

Thomas replied under his breath. "She paid her way through law school. I didn't say she was an idiot. Very rich lawyer indeed."

I was wondering why she didn't try to take you for child support."

"Hell, her family was filthy rich. I was the one begging because my father disowned me due to my involvement with her. He couldn't stand the family."

"Like Romero and Juliet?"

"Close to it, but Romero decided to heed his father's advice and leave Juliet alone pregnant with child and Juliet decided never to speak to Romero again and curse his name for the rest of her life."

Entering a conference room that sat twelve, five other people were gathered. Lester went over to an elderly man who looked about eighty and whispered something to him, then nodded at Thomas who approached them. Thaddeus stayed back near the door not wanting to intrude on the family that was now gathering around Thomas. The room carried voices to him though.

Newborn introduced Thomas to Clay Parsons, Agatha's fifth and last husband, Darlene Parson, Evelyn Cross, and Emmit Powell, her children all below the ages of twenty-two Darlene being the youngest at twenty. No one was familiar with Thomas except Clay who seemed to not take kindly to Thomas. The mousy-looking man with a thin frame was rather brusque saying out loud, "I don't even know why she invited you, she detested you greatly, sir."

"Love and hate are almost the same," Thomas rebutted. "Some people don't know the difference."

That shut him up pretty quick and even the others looked at Thomas now with some wariness. This may be from remembering Agatha saying the same thing all the time.

Newborn called the meeting to order, insisting everyone sit down so they could start the proceedings. "I will now start the reading of the will for Agatha Evelyn Washington Powell Cross Parson."

Thaddeus half listened watching mostly Thomas reaction to everything. The man was perfectly relaxed as Newborn read out what her children would receive, then her husband and her law partners. Thaddeus also noted confusion on some of the children's faces and even Clay's face.

Clay decided to speak up. "My wife was worth over seventy million dollars. She owned a fairly amount of large properties over half you've only mentioned. I don't understand what is to be left with the rest of the properties unless this asshole has something to do with it."

"You know your own, Clay?" Thomas asked seething.

Clay stood up. Newborn shouted his name before something ghastly popped out his mouth. "Please Mr. Parson, sit down. All will be known in due time."

Clay bristled under his breath. Darlene tried to quietly calm her father down, but her eyes could not stop wondering to the dark handsome stranger in the corner who had come with Thomas.

"At this time it is instructed by Agatha to stop the will reading and to read out loud a letter she prepared two days before her

death, which she gave to me the last time I saw her." He reached
into a large manila envelope and pulled out a pink smaller envelope. "I would like you, Clay, to verify this is your wife's familiar
stationary and that the seal is not broken and the signature underneath the seal is Agatha's true handwriting."

He took the envelope smelling it, closing his eyes taking a
whiff of his wife's essence still present in the fabric of the paper.
Without even looking it over, he knew it belonged to his Agatha.

"I verify." He handed the envelope back.

Newborn broke the seal and took out a two-page letter.

Thomas,

*You and I both know in our youth we made a lot of mistakes.
Especially with each other. We loved deeply, but we allowed our destinies
and family to get in the way of fate when we both knew we should have
not done what we did in the first place, but after it was done, we should
have faced our responsibilities and married. I for one agree what we did
was sin and I refuse to go to my death with that on my conscious.*

*I have made my peace with everything and everyone except you. The
only way I know I can do this is to give you peace that has bothered you
for years.*

The location of our daughter.

*My mother made the arrangements with a lawyer named Heaven
Wineguard. She won't release the records because she won't admit that
she lost these records. My mother took them purposely. She never wanted
either one of us to ever know where the child was, but before she could
securely hid them, she died and I located them. Our child was named
Laskie Smith. Do not ask me why or how that name came into play
with our daughter, but in Heaven's records the child is referred to as this
name. A household outside of Chicago adopted her. The adopting parents died and the child was basically lost in the system. The story is
much too long to go into right now and you will see the records soon
enough. I sent a private investigator that has just returned to me on my
deathbed to let me know that the child who is now twenty-three was
last located in Ohio where she ran away at a very young age. I hate that*

my child lived a horrible life like the one the investigator's report says she did—which you will also see soon enough—because I know I could have made her life just a little easier. I am not saying I should go to hell because of this, but I do say I should have done more. More than most since I knew a long time of her supposed whereabouts. Make it all right Thomas, even if you hate my guts as I have always hated yours for going with your father's decisions in your life and not your hearts. Make it right in her life. Give her the world once you find her and give her a hug only a true mother and father could give her. Thank you. Agatha formerly Soliel.

The room was strangely quiet as Newborn passed the letter to Thomas who looked roughly through the letter. Underneath her signature it read, "Stop reading." Underneath that was a P.S.

I did love you my whole life, but as you've always said to me, I could never tell the difference between hate and love. I know now that I just never wanted to believe I loved you. Believe this and love my daughter as we both were there. Yours in life and death.

He sighed rubbing his eyebrows rather disturbed by the letter.

Newborn began to read the rest of the will at this time. "I, Agatha Washington, being of sound mind and body leave the remaining property not mentioned about in the sole owner-ship of Laskie Smith, my first child born out of wedlock with Thomas Blair. In addition to this, I leave ten million dollars to Ms Smith and a trust fund of one million to be divided up between any off springs she might have produced." The will went on to accurately list the eleven holding all over the world that Ms Smith would obtain and in addition to this, the stocks of large billion dollar companies that would now be transferred to her name. Whoever this Ms Smith was now was a wealthy woman. So who was she? "In the event that Ms Smith has deceased the estate left to her will go to any and all off springs. In the event there are no off springs, the estate will return to the law offices as permanent to the business which then will go into the Newborn and Washington Scholarship fund."

Thaddeus thought this rather strange. She was set upon not leaving her new husband or any of her children anything than what she had already given them. Maybe because she felt in her heart she was wrong to give them anything when she had not been a real mother in the beginning.

Guilt made people do crazy things. Agatha was feeling plenty guilty. He prayed Thomas would have the chance of finding her before it was too late. Hopefully it was not.

Chapter 14

Completely frustrated she paced the room until Dr. Himes entered. He seemed almost disturbed as she was. Obviously he knew that she was seriously bothered. "The nurse has informed me you are not happy with the experimental birth control substance we have give you. Please tell me what is the problem?"

"What is the problem?!" she exclaimed almost hysterically. "I am completely thrown off track. I want my life back to normal. This 'experimental drug' is doing things to me that I don't think I can handle at this point in my life. I just moved here, I am having these weird dreams about a man I don't know—well I've briefly met . . ." she became flustered. "I-I . . . and I think I'm sleep walking. I've never done this before in my life. I don't know how to feel or what to do. I can't take it anymore."

"Calm down, please," he insisted. Pushing the intercom he called for Dr. Harry Potter. He was very worried Skye would start becoming like the other patients and with her being the more successful one it would be a blow to their finances and plans. "Have a seat," he urged.

"I don't want to have a seat and I certainly don't want to calm down." She began to yank at her hair pulling large handfuls from her scalp and not caring about the pain. It was better than the mental pain. Anything was better than the mental pain. "I want you to get whatever you put in me OUT!" She was screaming at the top of her lungs and she couldn't stop herself from yanking her hair until blood began to run down her forehead.

Dr. Potter entered the room looking quite concerned. He heard the gist of the last part outside the office because she had raised her voice so high the tone was more like screeching. In his pocket he brought a syringe of Thorazime and also some Valium.

"Ms Patterson, as I told you before the substance lasts for three months. You've just gotten to the second month. After the third month, we can—"

"I swear I'll go crazy!" She paced frantically like a caged animal. "You don't know how it is. You don't know." Finally she sat down or rather fell back on the couch near Dr. Potter, who slowly sat down beside her as not to startle her back to hysterics. She seemed worn and tired. There were dark circles around her eyes, her hair was all over her head, and her clothes were wrinkled and dirty. She really did look as if she were going to lose what little sanity she was holding on to.

"Ms Patterson, my name is Dr. Harrison Potter. I invented the birth control, I swear to you it won't cause any pain."

"I'm hallucinating. I've never hallucinated in my life. Even after everything. I've never dreamed so much in my life as I'm doing now and it's just one specific dream, it just changes slightly and gets longer. I can't explain it." She buried her face in her bloody palms and rocked back and forth. Those images began to fly through her mind again. The tingles began to flutter through her belly. No! No!!

"I insist you take these." Dr. Potter moved closer holding two Valium in his hand.

She slowly looked up at the doctor. When he entered she didn't pay any attention to him. He was just another white coat then, but now, she was looking into eyes that were familiar. She knew this man from . . .

Skye slapped the pills across the floor and shot to her feet. "I DON'T NEED ANYTHING, BUT PEACE OF MIND AND I WON'T GET IT UNTIL YOU GET THIS POISON OUT OF MY SYSTEM!!"

"Ms Patterson!" Dr. Himes called when she swung her arm again and knocked the lamp off the table near the couch.

She turned to verbally lash out at him, then suddenly felt a sharp pain in her buttocks. In the next instant she was surrounded by blackness.

Harry caught her just as she fell back and sighed in relief. She was light, but as old as he was, she was still a load. Dr. Himes assisted him in getting her back to the couch. The nurse came in. "Is everything alright, Doctors?" she asked concerned.

"Yes," Dr. Himes assured her ushering her out the room. "Ms Patterson is under a lot of mental strain. Can you send the resident for my next appointments? I want to attend to her personally and go into conference with Dr. Potter and Dr. Carter."

"Yes Doctor." The nurse left. Dr. Himes locked the doors and pressed mute on his phone to not be disturbed. While he did this, Dr. Potter took her temperature and blood pressure, which were normal. "How is she?" Dr. Himes asked as he watched Dr. Potter clean the blood from Skye's hands and face with a handi-wipe.

"She really needs the sleep. These dreams are bothering her. Why don't you prescribe her a low dosage of Valium? It shouldn't hurt us and it will calm her better when she is facing reality. It must be difficult to accept what is happening to her when she's never experienced it before. We shouldn't have tried it so soon."

Dr. Carter entered the room using his keys. He'd heard the last part of Dr. Potter's statement.

"She's perfect. Fats and I would not have it any differently. The nurse informed me of everything. How is she?"

"Emotionally and physically distraught and tired. I don't think this was a good idea considering her past. She is-"

"Enough!" Dr. Carter snapped. "Your medical knowledge on the female psychological state has much to be refuted, Doctor. We really don't want to hear you ramble about what detriment we are putting this young lady through. The Valium should be enough to curb the hysterics. Send her home with a prescription to hold her until it's time for her next shot, then we can administer another dose while she's under the influence, giving her a continuous refill on the valium."

"It'll make her into a drug addict!" Dr. Potter protested. "She will become a manic depressive."

"It is the only way to keep her under control. We cannot have these outbursts. The longer we keep her calm the longer we can use her to get more money for the studies. Its all in the name of science."

"Have you forgotten that this is a human being? We can't control her like a robot."

"That was the whole idea, Harry, or have you forgotten?" He didn't wait for Dr. Potter to respond, but pointed out another factor of their dilemma. "I haven't forgotten a thing and I surely haven't forgotten we received a large amount of money to produce your drug from Fats. If you're thinking about not going ahead with this you will be sorry."

Dr. Himes looked slightly past both of the doctors to the couch to see Skye slowly coming out of it.

"I think we need to discuss this outside the office and deal with her now," Dr. Himes said calmly.

"There's nothing to discuss. We have done too much and wasted enough time on her as I've said many times before. She will be fine and if not, there are now hundreds of other women I will have very soon which can do what she does successfully. If I have to I will use all of them to my advantage." He slammed out the room.

"His financial advantage," Dr. Potter sneered under his breath.

Dr. Himes went over to the couch to check on her. She seemed still unconscious, although he would swear a few minutes ago she was coming to.

Dr. Potter asked concerned, "Will she be alright?"

"A slight headache and soreness where we stuck her will be her case. Don't worry. The prescription should do just fine with the hallucinations. Let's let her rest," he insisted.

"Wait a minute, Neil, why did you get into all of this? Be honest with me."

"I am a doctor. Improving ways for stopping pregnancy was high on my list. Working with you came second."

"But now?"

He turned to meet Dr. Potter face to face. "But now, I don't think going about this way was right for the subjects. You are right; Dr. Carter is out for the money that we all will potentially earn. Let's just get our money and get the hell out of here. Let him work out this mess."

"What about the plans? The new subjects?"

"They are his plans and his subjects. Let's leave them like that. Infecting—which is what we are doing—these women with that hallucinogenic birth control was wrong. You and I both know, because we saw it here again today, but Dr. Carter can't see past the nose on his face or his bank account. All he sees is the money. We made a big mistake letting him in on the project, but you and I both know if it had not been for his underground connections we wouldn't have gotten the funding we needed for this whole thing, yet now we realize it came at a price bigger than we could pay back. We should just get our money and get the hell out of here."

"What about the patient's upstairs? What about her?"

"There is nothing we can do. I'm getting the money and leaving. If you want to sympathize you go ahead, but I refuse to spend my last days locked up in some jail for the rest of my life. I'm going to be on the farthest beach away from here."

Dr. Potter didn't know what to think or what to do. They had dug their graves and now they must lie in them. "Let's get her some rest and have the nurse check up on her in a few minutes."

Dr. Himes agreed following him out closing the door behind them.

As soon as they left, Skye sat up ready to panic again. It had been difficult keeping her breathing steady while the doctors were in the room. When she came out of the blackness from the sound of loud angry voices, she forced herself to not move a muscle when she knew heard what the voices were saying.

Valium indeed! She would be a walking drug addict like the ones she typed about all the time. Slowly getting up, she felt the soreness where the needle had stuck her, but got over the pain quickly knowing she didn't have enough time to dawdle. Gathering her things, she went out the office where it connected to a patient waiting room. She remembered this was the room she had been in initially when Dr. Himes had given her the first dose. Skye remembered the cabinet the drug had been in. Going over there now, she tried to open the small metal door, but it was locked. Looking through the other drawers she couldn't find a key, and then remembered he had pulled it out of his long white jacket.

Walking back into Dr. Himes office she looked on the back of the door. She knew he didn't have his medical jacket on when she came in the room. The Lord was with her, because he had not put it on when he had left. The keys were in there. Running back into the patient room, she quickly found the key and opened the cabinet. Taking two of the twenty vials in there, she closed the cabinet back and replaced the keys back in the jacket. Sticking the vials in her purse she proceeded to an emergency exit that was right outside the patient waiting room door. The other way would lead to the nurse's station. Before going through the emergency exit, she noticed an emergency stairway door near there and decided to enter that door instead curiosities gnawing on her mind like a hungry dog wanting a bone. Dr. Potter had said upstairs were more patients like her. What did he mean by that? What she was or what she would become?

The second level wasn't lit. Being noontime, the windows provided ample light down the long hallway and the floor was so quiet it was as if no one was up there. There was a long hall and about six doors on each side of the hallway. Looking through the first she saw a break room or a very small cafeteria, but then she noticed the straps on the chairs and a cold chill went down her spine. Moving further down the hall she looked in the rooms. The first two were empty, but the third one she came to, a girl who looked like she was in her teens was lying on the bed. She looked unkempt and obviously screaming or shouting from the way her mouth moved, but the room was sound proof. She was strapped to the bed writhing as if she was in a lot of pain. Going to the fourth door, the female in there looked in a more dejected state. The room was padded with no furnishings. The woman who looked to be about in the early thirties wore a straight jacket. She was rubbing the side of her face up against the walls. Skye saw other patches on the wall and marks all over her face of raw skin. There was a dazed look in her eyes as if she didn't see anyone, but something. Something put the weirdest smile on her face. There was no reality in her eyes and Skye had the feeling there would never be for the rest of her life or as long as the doctor's choose to keep her alive in misery. As she proceeded to the next rooms, each scenario worsened. Either the woman was spaced out or mentally deranged screaming and/or crying out their frustrated states of mind. The attention they were all in did not look like they were getting good medical condition and when she looked at the charts next to the doors she found that each one had a number. It started at four and ended at fifteen. This made her wonder what happened to one through three. Either way, Skye had a feeling one of those first two empty rooms was for her if she took another dose of that stuff.

If she didn't hightail her butt out of there, they would lock her up just because she really did know too much. Dr. Carter had a list filled with women, she remembered. Women, who after checking their backgrounds, could disappear without a trace. Skye was one of them and this terrified her. She realized once they were done with test subjects, the doctors put them up in these rooms. How long they kept you here or how long you lived after that was a mystery, but once the patients were gone, no one knew or cared.

Going back down the steps, she decided not to leave. Suspicion would be too great and went back on the couch. Sitting down in time as the other door opened with a nurse coming in carrying a glass of water and some pills.

"You're up? Good." She set the tray on the coffee table as she had a seat. "The doctor asked me on check on you earlier, but I was so busy I couldn't get around. Have you been up long?"

"No, I just sat up." Skye looked out her peripheral vision and noticed she had not closed the door to the other room. Since the nurse back was to this door, Skye was a bit relieved and hoped she could keep the nurses attention until she could get out the room.

"The doctor insisted you take these to help you and here is

your prescription to be taken twice a day. There are three refills and if you need some more, feel free to call the office and I will make sure you get whatever you need." She handed Skye a bottle of Valium with thirty pills inside.

The nurse waited while Skye looked down at the pills she was just handed. Putting the capsule in her mouth slowly, she tucked the pill under her tongue then sipped the water throwing her head back and pretending to swallow.

"That's a good girl."

"I should be getting home."

The nurse agreed. "Sure. Do you feel alright?"

She tried her best to sound grateful when she wanted to slap this woman and go into hysterics again. "I feel better. Thank you."

"Fine. Would you like me to help you to your car or call you a cab?" The nurse went behind the door and grabbed Dr. Himes jacket.

Skye shook her head while putting on her jacket and hurriedly walked out the office, before the nurse noticed the open door to the other room. "I'm fine," she said relieved as the nurse followed her out into the hallway. "Have a good day."

Once in her car, she took a deep breath. For some reason she felt she was still being watched. There was a juice bottle with a smidgen of juice left. The Valium was starting to dissolve under her tongue and she needed to get the pill out right away without them seeing her spit it out. Picking up the bottle she pretended to drink the juice, but instead spit the Valium out into the liquid.

As she drove off, she knew she had to do something right away. This was too big for her to handle. The list she had stolen the other night was the list Dr. Carter was referring to with the women names. They were going to drug them and carry on more experiments. The same ones they were doing on her without her even knowing.

*   *   *

Getting in the house, she decided to delve more deeply into researching the birth control they were using on her. She would go
into her medical dictionary and find out exactly what could the
birth control contained, then find the contact Dr. Welch knew
who could do the tests on the sample she had taken.

Until she knew everything she would try to stay calm and
keep her feelings under control much better. Her panic attacks
weren't getting *that* bad anymore, and if she just didn't lose her
mind, she would be almost normal.

Chapter 15

"You are wondering again," Thomas noted. "It's because of Melissa and Nicole isn't it?" Before Thaddeus could answer Thomas apologized. "I know I should have told them they weren't invited knowing it would make you this uncomfortable, but they are just as close as any of my other friends, Thad. Plus, she is your sister."

"Unfortunately," he said sarcastically. "I've finally figured out why they get along so well. Birds of a feather truly do flock together. I wasn't thinking about those two conniving women. I do have other things to think about."

"Like who? You have been mentally distracted this entire trip. Not as talkative as you usually are to me. Matter of fact, I've heard you talk more on the phone than you do to me of late. It's as if you're finding work to do instead of taking it easy."

"I have? Well, my new employee has really taken my interest. I needed an excuse to keep her busy so I could . . . spend more time with her."

"What kind of interest?" Thomas curiosity was clearly piqued.

"She's rather quiet, aloof . . . I don't know, but when she looked at me . . ." He was thinking of the day in the parking lot. "It was as if she looked right through me. It felt . . . strange."

"Disheartening is what you mean. You are so use to women looking with interest, the first one to not show it, makes you distracted. Hell, I should have clued Nicole in on that one."

Thaddeus chuckled knowing Thomas was pulling his leg. Thomas wanted Thaddeus married- happily married, and they both knew Nicole wanted to be that woman badly. She had asked Thomas several times how to go about getting Thaddeus, which was why she was getting close to Melissa. It would be possibly the only way to get in Thaddeus proximity—unless she tried Trisha, but he had a feeling the stuck up broad wouldn't lower herself to even speak to Trisha.

Thomas probed further quite interested in the young man's feelings. "What is her name?"

"Skye. She's rather plain you could say." He was only speaking of his experience in the parking lot. "But it's rather confusing. I've only seen her a couple of times, but I have spoken with her on several occasions, and I find her very intriguing. Maybe it's her mind, maybe I really need to get a life and I'm just grasping at air." He shook his head trying to get Skye off his mind, but he had been trying to do this since he met her and this trick didn't work either. Nothing would, it seemed to appease his curiosity about the woman. "I don't know, but I do know she has caught my interest and it's not just a simple matter. I'm also involved in a case where I find myself rather attracted to the case you could say. I can't really go into details about it. I am in a tizzy about who I really like."

"It seems you like one for the mind and the other for the body."

"You think? I come to that same conclusion myself."

Thomas answered, "It should cause confusion emotionally, because you are wishing it were the same person."

"Never. Skye could never be the Case."

"The case doesn't have a name?"

"I hate to admit, I haven't asked. She's always found a way to distract me. Pity isn't it?"

"Not only that, she does it quite well. You've always been a very focused man. I've never known you to daydream."

Again he repeated, "You think?"

"I know."

They both chuckled at their word play. "So is this Skye even interested in you mentally?"

Thaddeus shrugged. "I think. I have to force myself to stay safe with her. She's had it a little rough around the edges compared to

Melissa and Nicole, but other than that, I do believe she enjoys talking with me, although it's only been through e-mailing."

"So why don't you call her and just talk. If she feels uncomfortable, then go back to e-mailing, but you should try to let her know how you feel. If she is as intriguing as you say, it's a million and one chance you'll ever meet another girl like her. It takes a lot to intrigue you, Thaddeus and now that you've found her, you should try to pursue. You did express last time we spoke on this, you were seriously thinking of settling down, but only with the right woman."

"And what should I do about my feelings for the Case?"

"If it doesn't work out, at least you have the Case. It would be something if the Case and Skye were one and the same wouldn't it? That would be a good thing for you."

"Damn right," Thaddeus heartedly agreed.

Again they laughed earnestly about the subject. Thaddeus decided to change the subject slightly as he pondered on how he would speak to Skye next time they spoke. "Do you have any plans of getting married, Thomas?"

"I think right now, I would like to just concentrate on finding my daughter and giving her some kind of happiness that she probably never really had. For some reason I feel I can make her life complete by finding her and letting her know I was a stupid young man, and I have always loved her."

Thaddeus knew whoever this girl was would be the luckiest woman in the world with her mother's inherited fortune and a father like Thomas who would adore her. He prayed for Thomas' good journey and hoped the man would find his daughter. Standing up, he decided to retire for the night.

Thomas knew he was only going to connect with his laptop to e-mailing the woman he called Skye. He prayed Thaddeus would find true unconditional happiness in his life. If this was the woman Thaddeus wanted, Thomas also prayed she would love the young man as much as he would love her.

*   *   *

Skye rubbed her eyes. Deciding to finish up her largest account before going to sleep had been a good idea for her peace of mind. It kept her distracted. Right after she had left the doctor's office she made a long distance call to Dr. Welch in Davenport. He told her there was a laboratory on the eastside he knew of where she could go and get something analyzed. He would call ahead for her and have his friend, John Dandridge be on the lookout for her. After speaking with John he was quite disturbed by the vial and promised to give her a call or fax her the results of his study in a day or two.

Once she was finished, she went online to send the reports over. After the e-mail was sent, she received two messages. One was junk mail, and the other was from Thaddeus Newman.

I will be calling you about eleven tonight, please stay by the phone. Reply if you are unable to keep this appointment.
TN

Skye stared at the screen for a good minute wondering why would he want to speak with her personally. Usually when the main client called there was a problem with the account. She really didn't need this now. She wondered if she canceled would he just have Trisha call. Deciding not to hit REPLY was hard, but she didn't and waited. Shutting down her computer, cleaning up downstairs, and then taking a nice hot shower at 10:59 the phone rung.

"Is there a problem?" she immediately asked not even saying hello.

"Why would there be a problem?" he asked curiously.

"Bosses never call unless there is."

"There isn't, now what?"

"That's what I would like to know." She was becoming upset.

He could sense her frustration and decided to relax her. "Am I calling too late?"

"Never. You are a client."

He paused a little. "What if I told you I would like to be more than a client?"

She didn't get it. "Are you offering me a job as an employee?"

"No, I was offering friendship."

Those butterflies started up again in her stomach. She could not believe this was a social call from Thaddeus Newman. Things like this didn't happen to ordinary woman. 'Lord, was this another dream?' She looked to the bedside for the Valium. Should she take some? "I don't know what to say."

He didn't figure he'd strike her speechless. "It's either yes or no."

"Or why would be a good answer."

"No that would be a question to answer a question. That's not good at all."

She almost laughed, but wasn't sure if he was kidding with her or not. "Can my question be answered?"

He heard the humor in her voice and relaxed. "I've come to realize that you are very nice to speak with. Not just professionally, but on a personal level as well. I've been thinking a lot about you even though I've only met you fully once. I know from our brief talks that I would enjoy speaking with you more."

That was a mouthful, but it was enough to knock her speechless. She took a moment to gather her thoughts. He wanted to get to know her better? No, not him—she was definitely dreaming. "Let me get this straight, you enjoy our talks even though they have only been brief and unemotional, and you want to get to know me better, yet you've only really met me once and really only know me on a professional level."

"There are the e-mails. You say this like it's too good to be true."

Her tone was sharp. "Mr. Newman, not only is it too good to be true, I don't believe one ounce of it and I think I need to go find my boots because there's enough crap floating around to overflow my house."

"So you think I'm up to something?"

"Are you?"

"No. I'm sincerely and honestly offering friendship."

"Friendship?"

"Yes, just friendship. Nothing more. I thought I could be open and honest with you, and you would maturely take-"

She cut him off. "Maturely? You don't think I'm being mature about this?"

"I don't think you take me seriously enough."

"I don't think you have thought this through. I think you're thinking about the moment or many moments. Hell, I don't know what you're thinking, but it's definitely not sane. You can't possibly want to be my friend."

He took offense at this. "Why not?" She was classifying him like he was classifying his sister and Nicole. Yes, it was unfair for him to do so, but he couldn't believe she was stereotyping *him*. "I enjoy talking to you."

"Why? When we constantly debate over issues that don't make a difference to the prices of all the tea in China."

He was about to say forget the whole thing when he couldn't help his laughter. She looked at the phone oddly then put it back to her ear. "You've really lost your mind."

"You've just explained it. Why wouldn't you be friends with me when we get along so well?"

Huffing, rolling her eyes heavenwards, she thought the man was one beer short of a six-pack. "I think this could ruin our professional career."

"No it won't I think we are both mature to separate that from our friendship."

"We are?"

"Indeed."

She was quite leery about this entire situation. The man she was having fantasies about was the same man on the phone with her at this moment. How was she not to feel suspicious when all her other reality was crumbling around her? Yet, she wanted it. She wanted to tell him everything. She needed a friend like him.

He would be able to understand her and even believe her. At that moment, she wanted to spill her guts, but just as the moment was building up to doing so, she changed her mind at the pinnacle. "I think this is too much." She fought the panic attack rising.

He never expected that response. "Too much? I'm too much?"

"Yes . . . No . . . This—this thing . . ."

"Friendship," he finished.

"Yes. Yes!" The butterflies were getting worse. "How am I suppose to be friends with you without thinking about . . ." She gasped pressing the receiver to her chest and closing her eyes fighting the memories again. In this one he was holding her, kissing her, and his mouth was so hot, his tongue so moist and strong. Biting her lip from the pure sensation of knowing she could feel this way if he did this to her was overwhelming, but it felt so wicked. Opening her eyes and calming down she brought the receiver back to her ear.

Quietly, she said, "hello."

"Are you alright?" he asked genuinely concerned.

Nodding at the same time, she said, "Yes, I think."

"You were saying something about how are you suppose to be friends with me without thinking about what?"

"I don't know." She paused another moment to gather her thoughts. Having a panic attack about now would certainly be quite disturbing for him. 'Now just get it together Skye and breathe. If you just breathe you can do this.' "I just feel very overwhelmed at this moment. You really are a nice man, Mr. Newman, and offering friendship is a great honor because I believe deep inside you are serious about this, yet I can't figure out why me?"

"I've told you."

"Yes, you've thought about me and all that, but there has got to be something more."

"Maybe that is what I'm trying to figure out myself and I just haven't gotten over the wall to see why. Maybe I need to somehow connect to you first, to realize what I really want from you. I don't want to use you. I truly do want to become closer through friendship, Ms Patterson. Is this possible?"

Closing her eyes again and laying back on the bed to relax herself, she answered, "Yes." After another pregnant silence she said, "When you find out will I be the first to know?"

"Oh most definitely. I wouldn't dare tell the press before I gave you at least a hint."

This time she did let out a tickled huff. He was yanking her chain.

"Did I make you smile all the way this time?" he asked.

"Yes," she blushed biting the corner of her lip.

"Try to let me know when I do, because you hide your emotions so well. I'm not use to experiencing that from women." He made himself relax feeling the doubt and distrust going away from her. This was crazy, but he felt like he could now tell her anything. She had accepted his friendship and that was a step in the right direction. "Now that we are friends, I think we need to make rules."

She tensed a little wondering was this the point when she found out his ulterior motive. "What kind of rules?"

"The kind where we know when and where to be friends, what subjects we can and cannot talk about, and so forth."

"Why don't we make them up as we go? That way we can go so far, then know when to stop without worrying about not being ourselves and honest with each other, but also not limit us when we get to a peak of understanding in our relationship."

His mind was blown! She had a deeper sense of people and to become her friend was a big step for her and him. He knew being close to her would be entering Eden for the first time. Looking at the world through her eyes could be the best experience of his life. It would be something he would cherish for the rest of his life. To make light of her statement, he said, "You seem quite the friendship maker."

Again she laughed that breathless laugh, stirring his senses as it had the first time she had done it. "This is my first real one, I guess. I've had associates and such, but not a very real friend who just asked me outright. It's different. What do friends like us do?"

Though coming from her, the question was filled with innocence, yet he didn't think innocently. "Talk, do things together, I guess. We can just make it up as we go along with that as well."

"One rule we should say right now is we need to be honest with each other. I have too much going on in my life for games, Mr. Newman."

"I couldn't have said it any better. I'll insert a rule at this time too. We can call each other by the first names at our convenience."

"Our convenience?" she questioned. "When is that?"

"When we feel comfortable."

"I take it you don't like me calling you Mr. Newman?"

"I think it's very formal for friends, yet I don't want to make you feel uncomfortable by insisting upon it."

"I will concede and say I will try." A yawn escaped her lips.

"I think I have bored you enough."

"Bored me? Oh yeah," she teased. "You are hardly boring, Mr . . ." she sighed. "Yes, I do think that it will be hard to call you anything other than Mr. Newman. Getting comfortable with friends will take some getting use to. After a while, I know I won't be so nervous with you as I feel right now. Are you a patient man?"

"For you of course. I do feel comfortable calling you Skye."

Small goose bumps came on the back of her neck at the sound of hearing his voice say her name. She wondered if he knew how sensuous he sounded sometimes.

"Can I ask you a personal question?" he asked.

She shrugged seeing no harm in this. "I guess."

There was an impregnable pause, before he asked, "What are you doing while you're talking to me?"

"Thinking about what I'm going to say next."

He chuckled. "No. Where are you? In front of your computer?"

"No, sometimes I do other things than sit in front of my computer, you know."

He knew she had taken a small offense at this remark. "I know, but every time I imagine what you're doing or think about what you're doing, I picture you sitting in front of your computer with your hair drawn up in a tight bun, layers of clothes on from neck to ankle and those god-awful glasses pressed against your nose. I guess because I don't know what else you like to do. Can I know?"

She was flabbergasted he had thought about her in such detail. "I like my computer. I like my work. I go shopping, but I have phobias you could say. I don't trust too many people, so I don't socialize, but recently I did have a small excursion out on the town with a person who knew an associate of mine in Ohio. We went to the Karaoke bar in Greektown. It was quite nice."

"Did you sing?"

"Do pigs fly? I don't think so."

He laughed quite enjoying her sarcasm. "You know you still didn't answer my question."

"Oh yes. I'm in my room about now, getting ready to sleep. I do that sometimes." She was purposely being sarcastic from his crack about her always at her computer. "What are you doing?"

"I've decided to stay up late and do some work. I have some stocks over in China and I like to watch them at night occasionally, which is when the market is opened. I need to catch up on some reading as well."

"Do you ever sleep?"

"Sometimes. I have a hard time sleeping when I have so much on my mind unless I tire myself out. I know that might sound strange. I love Thomas like a father. I should feel quite relaxed here, but sometimes when his guest come, I don't." He had mentioned Thomas earlier in his e-mails to her so she knew and understand how close they were if she actually read the e-mails.

"What guest?"

He smiled knowing since she didn't question about Thomas, she had read his e-mails. "His niece, by marriage, named Nicole has been trying to hoodwink me into getting back in a relationship with her."

She tried to make her question sound formal. Skye didn't want to seem like she was being nosey or really cared whom he dated. "What was the reason for her departure in your life in the first place?"

"She decided to marry me."

"What was wrong with that?"

"I didn't ask her or even know about the wedding until a month before the big event and that was because Craig asked me where were my bachelor party festivities going to take place."

She tried to keep from laughing. "That would be hard to explain, wouldn't it? I can just imagine the pillow talk. 'Guess what honey, we're getting married tomorrow.'"

Thaddeus let out a loud burst of laughter he was sure the bedroom occupants next to him heard. Skye joined his mirth on the other end of the phone. He had never had a sense of humor about the entire "Nicole-situation," but this diamond in the rough had teased him dangerously about it.

"I shouldn't tease you about something that must have been quite painful to know. She outright deceived you and that's certainly no laughing matter."

"It's fine. I must admit it's the first time I've laughed about it. Thank you so much for giving me reason to."

"How long had you two been seeing each other?"

"About six months."

"It took her a six months to ascertain she wanted to spend forever with you?"

"She had nothing better to do than to plan a wedding. Her crowd considered me a good catch and she would be a fool to let me walk away."

"That's quite a cocky statement to make."

"It's not cocky, just over confident."

She let out a breathless chuckle again. "I guess you didn't bother to offer friendship first?" she asked surly.

Again he let out an earsplitting chortle tickled pink in her humor. He would have never imagined Skye had the wry wit just like his own, which he couldn't believe how much he enjoyed.

"She's gotten my sister, Melissa, in her good graces and both of them are here trying to pin me down."

"Why would your sister want to do that? She should want the best for you. I wouldn't understand her at all."

"Join the club. Melissa's agenda would be to find any and all ways to get her hands on more money. Would you believe she tried to sue me because she said since she helped me fill out my college application and study for the SAT's she was entitled to fifty percent of my life earnings?"

"That's crazy!" she gasped. "This is your real sister?"

"Half sister. She's been spoiled to death and she married for love and not for money and her husband turned out to be a loser, so instead of divorcing him she cheats on him and she tends to ignore him."

"Oh now that's a lovely marriage."

"I don't ever want to be married like that. I guess seeing my mother being married three times and my sister unhappy at love, it's made me rather aloof at marrying."

"I can understand that."

"What's your excuse?"

"My excuse for not being married?" She shrugged laying it out for him. "I guess the right guy hasn't asked me. I work too much. I don't go out to social very much, I have a smart aleck sense of humor that no one understands, but me, and of course the fact I was sexually abused when I was eleven does make it hard for me to be comfortable around men personally."

He was shocked to quietness. She was quite open about that, and had honestly told him something quite personal. Skye would clearly understand if he found a reason to hang up. Usually men did try to get away from her after she told them. It was as if she was a damaged good. "You were trying to make me hang up, weren't you?"

"I was only being honest," this was a lie and truth. That had been a test to see if he would find an excuse to hang up on her.

"But the brittle way you presented to me, was rather . . . shocking."

"True, but how else was I to say it?"

"We must work on your gentle side."

"Only for those I truly care about."

"Are there many of them out there?"

She paused hating to admit it, but knowing it was brutally true. "Maybe one or two."

Again Thaddeus was strangely quiet, but this one was different than a nothing to say quietness. He did want to say something, but didn't feel it was appropriate to say at this point. Urging him on, she asked, "What are you thinking about?"

"I don't want to pity you. You don't want that. I envy how you say it so calmly and have picked up the pieces going on with your life. That's admirable to know. I'm glad to have you as a friend Skye. You will teach me a lot about life."

She blushed making that huff laugh she always did he was becoming to identify as her hidden amusement. "I'm glad you are my friend too, Mr . . . um . . . Thaddeus."

This was encouraging for him and decided to go a bit further. "I plan to fly into town tomorrow for some business tomorrow night. I have all morning and afternoon free. Would you care to join me at the café where we first met?"

"I should think about it before I agree. Our friendship is so new. Meeting so early could jeopardize something, couldn't it?"

"I will give you a chance to think about meeting and call you about eleven tomorrow morning. Goodnight Skye."

She wanted to talk more, but would not admit her need for more conversation with him at that moment. "Goodnight, Thaddeus." She didn't want to push her blessings.

Putting the receiver down, she moved around until she was comfortable, curving the pillow into her body. That had been what she needed. A friend.

For the first in many days, she fell into a deep sleep.

*　　*　　*

He starred at the phone a good minute before he realized he was just staring at the receiver. Putting it down, he leaned back in his chair and absently logged on to his Internet account. That had been productive and the conversation hadn't hurt a bit. He was almost tempted to call her back despite the hour being past midnight.

Remembering what Thomas said about the Skye and the Case being the same was still on his mind as well. That would be his perfect woman, but for now, he would be content with this separation. Sex wasn't always important in a relationship and was an easy enough wall to conquer. Knowing Skye as a friend was important.

Chapter 16

The smell of lavender filled the room. Her back arched as the sensations engulfed her pelvis. She could feel the moistness between legs and if she grind her hips just a little more, yes, yes, *"Yes Thaddeus!"*

Awaking in bed drenched in sweat, she covered her mouth as if she were a child shouting a curse out loud to a parental unit. Looking around frantically, she almost felt as if the dream had been real. Too real. Someone had been here or there, or wherever the memory had come from. She had never had oral sex done to her in her entire life, so how could she experience something of that nature so clearly? Too clearly. True she knew about it, had written about it in her books, but never imagined something so vividly.

'No you will not go crazy. Not yet.' Looking at the clock, she read eight AM. She was a little groggy from staying up way past her bedtime, but she managed to get out of bed and get dressed.

Getting back in front of her computer, she went straight to the Internet. Today her goal was to find more out about Trisha's boyfriend. Skye remembered him being introduced as Alan Coleman. After thirty minutes of looking around with unsuccessful searches she decided to think about the other name Trisha called him. TREAVOR.

Typing this name in with Alan Coleman, the search was narrowed and she pulled up something interesting—TAC Enterprises. Searching around some more, she found out TAC Enterprises was presently under FBI investigation for money laundering from an article in the Detroit News. The president and CEO, Trevor Coleman, Sr. a.k.a. Cole Forsythe a.k.a. Fats in the underground market. There were many legal and illegal businesses TAC Enterprises had all over the world and many connections to other enterprises as well.

The time was almost eleven so she decided to get dressed for lunch. His call was again a minute early. "Are you hungry?" he asked after greeting her a proper good morning.

"You never said specifically why you're in town."

"I do have a business to run."

"Then why aren't you running it?" she asked flippantly wondering if he would understand her wit.

He did and shot right back at her, "I am also a master at multitasking. Are you making excuses not to go to lunch with me?"

"Oh of course not," she lied feeling he knew she was not being honest. "I don't want you to feel you are obligated to entertain me just because we're friends and you're in town."

"I am the one asking, aren't I?"

"Alright. I will meet you for lunch, but only if you promise we can go Dutch."

"That is what friends do. The café in thirty minutes?"

She confirmed, "till then, Mr. Newman."

"Till then," he reaffirmed stiffly irate by the formal name she reverted to again.

Driving to the café she wondered if she was crazy? No, this was just an attempt in her life to actually be mentally normal. She was living her fantasy. Skye knew she could deal with this if she didn't think about the so real dreams, yet she needed to talk about what was happening to her. Was it too soon to speak about this to him? She wondered to herself.

He was already there when she arrived five minutes early and stood up as she approached looking extremely handsome in a green Versace' three piece suit. She had worn a nice brown silk dressed ankle high with a matching jacket and an elegant scarf to wrap around her hair keeping it covered. Due to the extreme curliness of her long honey brown hair, she had little time to do something nice to it. She hated the difficult to manage curliness, because drying her thick hair took forever and her arms grew tired. Besides everyone was allowed to have a bad hair day, she just didn't want Thaddeus to see.

Thaddeus didn't feel nervous until she approached the table. Her eyes were expressionless just as he remembered, and kept lowered. He didn't know if this was on purpose. She greeted him with a firm quick handshake as she sat across from him. The waitress came over to them to take their order. Skye told her "Water, for now."

"You look traveled," she noted. Usually he received compliments, maybe even a nice hug or kiss, but a handshake and a "traveled?" What the hell does someone who looked traveled look like? He decided to ask.

She responded, "Tired, needing rest. Do you?"

"I don't think so. Are you trying to avoid having this lunch?"

"That is the second time you have insinuated that question."

"Is it true?"

"Yes, but I don't like you pointing it out."

Amused he asked, "What's so bad about having lunch with me?"

"Nothing," she lied.

"I think I smell something."

"What?"

He leaned closer to her. "Bullshit."

Skye giggled.

"What's so awful about me?" he asked sincerely.

She bit her lip knowing he had found the source of her uneasiness. "I'm just not comfortable with you. You're too much."

This was a new one. "What do you mean by too much?"

Exasperated, she said, "Your status, your position in life compared to mine, your looks, your height, your past. I could go on."

"The differences bother you?"

"Yes and no." She elaborated. "I'm honored by the friendship offered, but just the thought of being your friend is a lot to take in. I'll be privy to being in the company of Thaddeus Newman. A man I've only seen in papers or heard in news articles that I can actually say I know. I've never had a celebrity in my life and it just takes some getting use to."

"I don't consider myself a celebrity."

"I'm sure Denzel Washington says the same thing. I'm still not clear on the why me tip."

He looked down at her hand and moved a thumb unconsciously up and down the length of her pinkie finger as he looked up at her. "When I see something in my business life that just stands out, I go after it. I obtain it, and I come out a better person and a wealthier man. For the first time in my life, I found something in my personal life that stands out, Skye. You. There's an inner fire inside of you that I just can't explain, but I want to warm my soul near the warmth. You've opened my eyes, my heart, and my mind to an unbelievable experience."

Skye's breath caught in her throat as she snatched her hand away and held her palm as if the skin had been burned. Looking away from his face, she calmed her racing heart.

He chose his words carefully not wanting her to pull away emotionally as she just had physically. Sitting back a little, he spoke from his heart, "I . . . like you as person."

"A person?"

"I don't want you to feel that there is an underlying reason. Now can friends have lunch?"

She consented feeling a little better because he had changed the subject and ordered something light while he ordered as if he had not eaten in years. "Do you always eat heavy or is it just your size you please?"

"My size has nothing to do with it. I eat because I like the food here and I have no intentions of eating another meal until tomorrow. Maybe a snack tonight and tomorrow morning, but that will suffice until my flight Sunday night." He leaned close to the table, which he noted she sat away from with no direct eye contact, yet he had a need to receive it. She was giving him brief looks then directed her eyes to the side. "Does my size bother you?"

"Yes. You played sports didn't you?"

"I played football until a knee injury in college. Crap happens and you go on, right? So why does my size bother you?"

"Because you aren't average, you know this. It is rather intimidating."

He agreed taking her hand in his. "True, my size is rather intimidating, but I don't think it is anything to be feared. I like being this size, but I don't want you to ever fear me."

"You don't think I couldn't? Look how big your hands are to mine. You don't think I should be a little fearful?"

"I am a man, who is only human. I don't hurt people I care about and I especially wouldn't hurt my friends. Don't ever fear me, Skye."

She nodded. "I will try, but I won't make any promises."

He nodded. "Can I ask a favor?"

"We're friends, that is allowed."

"Look at me. The eyes are keys to the soul. Your soul is one I want to be close to. I need to see it to understand you better."

Slowly with a lot of effort, she moved her eyes to the deepest cinnamon eyes. He did want her to look at him, it showed clearly through his eyes. Quickly she lowered her head afraid she would start those hallucinations again. Reaching across the table he gently lifted her chin, until her eyes met his again.

"What happens once you understand me? Will you go away?"

"Never. You're stuck with my friendship for life. When I give my hand of friendship, it's not just something I want on a whim. I have associates and business relationships for that. When I offer friendship, it's because I want to be the ear you use, the shoulder you lean on, and the company you need when you just want company. In turn, I will only ask for the same. Your eyes are extraordinary. You never knew your parents at all or any relatives?"

She shook her head. "Never. I don't even know my birth date. I just celebrate it in January, because that is when I was turned over to the state."

"Does it bother you sometimes? Knowing you were abandoned?" he asked his deep voice filled with concerned.

She knew he only asked to find out more about her, but she wasn't sure if she wanted him to find out everything about her, because once he did his attention would turn elsewhere, even though he said it would not. Yet, to deny him information when he asked so honestly as if feeding him this would only make him want to know more, made it hard for her to deny him, so she knew she would tell him anything he wanted to know. "No, not anymore. I mean as a little girl, I dreamed of waking up one day and my parents came knocking at whatever foster home I was at to take me away. I use to scream when they told me I'd be moving to a new home, because I thought the more homes they moved me to, the harder it would take for my parents to find me. As I grew older, in my teen years, I would just wish for even one parent to come. A mother or a father, then I would just want an aunt, grandfather, someone, anyone." Her voice faltered a little, and she used the opportunity to sip a little water. "As soon as I turned sixteen, I went to the judge and received my independence. I'd been doing word transcribing for a while and my foster father had been taking every nickel and dime I made. I stopped looking for any semblance of family after I went to Chicago where it all started, but no one had any records I could get to. Everything was private as if no one wanted me to find out who created me, so I went on with life, but . . ."

"But what?" he asked eagerly enthralled by what she was telling him.

She leaned on the table, raising one hand up to rest her chin on the end of her palm. "As all girls, I wish for that something of a father to come into my life and be there. Dr. Welch in Davenport came close to it, but there is nothing like the real thing. My greatest wish from when I was a little girl is to walk down the aisle on my wedding day to the man I will love forever and look beside me to the man who has loved me from the beginning." She blinked away the pain. "It's just a dream, I guess. Only a dream." Then she muttered under her breath, "I've been having a lot of those lately."

Meeting Thaddeus's eyes again, she wondered what he was thinking and if he had heard her last comment. He looked doubtful. "I'm not sure what to say. I am unsure how to take this all."

She softly touched the top of his hand and smiled comfortingly. "Listen. Just listen." Small ripples of pleasure surged through her fingertips, up her arm and through her veins. She wondered had he felt the same from her touching him, but didn't ask.

The waitress broke the electricity between the, when she brought their food over. Skye withdrew her hand.

"Thank you for having lunch with me," he said when the waitress left.

"It's no problem. It's what friends do."

"I must admit all of this is very new to me. I've never had a female friend. Not even in high school."

"Will you be out of town long?"

"I'm traveling with a good friend of mine to Ohio to meet a lawyer about some personal business. We've been working on finding someone for about three years."

"Would that be Thomas Blair? I typed the letter last week."

"Yes it would be Thomas Blair. I'm mostly traveling with him for support. The mother of the child just died and finally released some vital information. We're going to search around and hope he finds what he is looking for."

"With all the time you put into it, I hope so too," she said wishing him well.

"You mentioned something under your breath having a lot of dreams. What did you mean by that?"

She flushed embarrassed to know he'd been paying close attention to her. "I've been having these dreams about being with someone. As wild as I know my imagination can be, I know I could never imagine something so clear. Like I'm really there."

Thaddeus heart began to beat faster, but he put the thought that raced through him behind. Impossible! Skye could not be part of Fats ring. Never could she be. "Do you do it often?"

"Every once in a while."

"May I be so bold to ask whom do you have dreams about?"

She hid her blush biting her lips fighting the flush covering her whole body. "It's no one," she quickly lied. "After my assault at a young age, I stopped dreaming."

"Stopped dreaming?" he frowned. "And recent events in your life have made you start? Could it have been the move?"

"I thought of that option to. Taking this step in my life was scary, but I knew it was something which had to be done." Her voice faltered wanting to elaborate more about the trouble she believe she could be in, but decided maybe next time she would. "It's confusing, but I want to make the best of this decision."

He took her hand in his and lightly brushed her knuckles with his lips. "I believe you have."

She gently took her hand away and changed the subject. As they ate, he noted everything about her, without seeming too obvious. Could she be apart of Fats ring and not know it. He wanted to know desperately, yet he didn't want to press her remembering how Dr. Powers said the fragile state of mind they could be in. His Skye? He couldn't fathom the thought, but remembering how the Case looked and his Skye he was becoming more aroused by the minute.

Deciding to separate the two in his mind, he concentrated on Skye. He wanted to get too much of her, so he could get just enough, but it seemed the more things he noted about her, the more he wanted to be with her, know about her, make her happy. This was crazy he knew, sitting here having lunch with her. He didn't know if he could have just come into town and not see her. Not after they had made so much progress last night.

When they were paying for the bill together, she asked, "I don't mean to waste what little time you have."

This time he put his finger to her lips to stop her. The movement was erotic and sweet at the same time. "Don't ever think you are a waste of time to me. If you were, I would let you now, don't you think?" As he spoke the tip of his finger traced the bottom of her lip. When he realized how intimate the touch was, he drew away instantly regretting what he had done.

She nodded stiffly trying to ignore the madness of emotions she was feeling. "As friends, I believe you."

"No matter how important I am to the world around us, when I make time for you, it means I want to be with you. I know I am not obligated, nor am I forced. I want to be here." Bad timing happened at that moment when his cell phone went off. To further his bad luck, it was Craig's contact telling him Craig needed to see him immediately at the apartment. Cursing under his breath, she already knew this meant he had to leave.

"I understand," she said, really meaning the words as she stood up. He followed her to her car feeling like an idiot. First, he said he wanted to be with her, then he had to leave when his phone went off. It didn't look good for the home team in his opinion.

"I'll try to call you before I leave tomorrow night," he promised. "Mind if I call you late?"

"No. It was a nice lunch . . . Thaddeus." She outstretched her hand. "Till the next time?"

"Promise. If you feel like talking any time, you can call me over at the River Place apartments. That's where I'm staying for now."

"Sure." Getting in her car, she took a deep breath wondering if she should be making a big deal about his work coming first. She was very understanding because she would do the same if it concerned her business.

Instead of going home, she went to the library to look through some more information on the doctors and TAC Enterprises. About five she found the connection between them, when TAC donated over half a million dollars to the study on GHB which Dr. Potter was in charge of. Now all she needed was to put the drug inside her of and Dr. Potter's secret study together. She was sure there was some law breaking taking place and charging whom ever with a crime would suit her just fine. She only wanted to stop the doctors before they injected more unsuspecting women.

She pulled up in her driveway to see Dr. Himes and Dr. Potter standing on her doorstep. It looked as if they were just getting there and looked please to see her. Warily she got out the car making sure she stuffed the papers she had made copies at the library deep in her purse hoping they wouldn't see.

"You didn't come in for you appointment, and we were worried," Dr. Himes explained.

"So you make house calls? Should I be honored or scared?"

"Both," Dr. Potter said seriously. "May we come in to speak with you, Ms Patterson?"

Their eyes spoke volumes and she had a feeling denying them would lead to more trouble. "Yes." She allowed them to follow her in the house. Putting her purse on a coffee table double-checking the closed zipper she offered them something cold or hot to drink.

Dr. Himes said nothing, but Dr. Potter asked for a cold tea.

Returning to see them with the paper from her purse she became highly upset. Skye grabbed the papers out of Dr. Himes hands. "How dare you!" she screamed furiously.

"How dare we? How dare you put your nose where it doesn't belong, Ms Patterson?" Dr. Potter pointed to the television where they had put a tape in showing hallway video surveillance on the second floor of her walking down the long aisle at the medical center dated yesterday peeking in the windows of each door.

"I-I was lost," she quickly lied. "I needed to use the bathroom. I didn't see anything."

"Would that be why you're looking for connections between Fats Coleman and us?" Dr. Himes asked nodding to the papers she gripped to her chest. "You may have not seen a lot, but we think you know enough."

Dr. Potter turned her around to look at him. "Maybe even too much and if Dr. Carter know how much you know . . ." He left the subject open.

"We want you to keep your mouth shut for your sake, Ms Patterson. You can't afford to open your mouth to anyone," Dr. Himes warned her from behind as he eyes were locked with Dr. Potters.

"You're a beautiful young woman, Ms Patterson." Dr. Potter cupped her cheek. His palm felt cold and sweaty. "I have worked decades to make my drug perfect and I will not have you make the last years of my life miserable behind bars. Do we make our point?"

She nodded slowly too terrified to speak.

Dr. Himes turned her towards him. "It won't be just us making the threats either if Dr. Carter ever finds about just how much you know. The money and the people funding this project are dirty. Real dirty and they have ways to make people like you disappear."

Dr. Potter pried the can of ice tea out her hands and opened it. "Good day, Ms Patterson." He sipped the drink down and placed the can back in her hand as Dr. Himes exited out the door before him then he followed.

Her legs buckled under her in terror. What had she gotten herself into? Rocking in trepidation, her mind scrambled for what to do next. With it being Saturday afternoon, she wasn't sure what to do.

'Stay calm,' she told herself. If only that was possible, then she would be able to live her life as if nothing had ever happened. Coming to Detroit had been a bad thing, she concluded, but she would have never met Thaddeus if she had not come here. This is not the time to think about him . . .

Maybe it was. Maybe she ought to let him know.

Tomorrow, she decided. Tomorrow when he called she would let him know everything. Right now she needed to be ready for anything. Getting up from the floor of her living room, she went to the front door and turned the dead bolt lock. Skye went straight upstairs and packed an emergency bag with extra clothes and food, plus traveler's checks she had left over from her trip to Detroit, important papers and extra cash. She made a copy of the files and reports she had been researching and stashed all this in the bag as well. Once she was done with that, she went in her backyard and stashed this in the doghouse, which had come with the house.

Trying to work that night was difficult, but soon she opted with a long bath at eight and bed. Too high strung, she reluctantly took a Valium promising herself she would toss them away in the morning. The idea of getting hooked on them made her terrified, but just tonight she would have to take them in order to get any kind of rest.

Dreamland hit her instantly with a strange ringing of the phone.

Chapter 17

Craig arrived two hours later looking paranoid as he came through the secret entrance of the apartment in the bedroom's closet. Thaddeus was about to speak until Craig made a silent gesture, then instructed him to follow him right back out the secret entrance. They walked down several flights of stairs until they got to the fourteenth floor. He followed him to a service elevator. Once inside, Craig pushed a basement button, but breathe a sigh of relief.

"It's bad, isn't it?" Thaddeus surmised from all of this.

"Pooh was found dead last night. His tongue and eyes had been literally ripped out his body. FBI called the sergeant and I up this morning. They believe it's Laroche Butts. He's worked for the mob out of a Chicago hit man squad. He's about seven feet and big as a Mack truck, but no one's stayed alive to pin him with anything yet. Except one cat knows his handiwork and they said this was his needlepoint."

"You think Fats called him in?"

"According to them, Chenile, Butts' daughter use to do some thing for Fats and Fats contacted her two days ago. She paid him off with her dad. Fats wanted to send a message to the police. He knows and I'm terrified of what's going to happen. I think you should cancel out tonight and get out of town until we can bring everyone in. It's going down tomorrow afternoon. We've got enough to connect Fats to this chain and all the doctors as well. Pooh received some good information on tape from Fats, and gave them to me day before yesterday. Fats was about to get him in on the deal, because Pooh knew of some women on a big list we have no idea about but heard it mentioned several times. We figured once we get all the parties involved, we'll get it out of someone, or at least stop them, but I think they've already started drugging new women already. The clinic was packed Friday with new patients which I believe were these women on this mysterious list. Pooh didn't have a chance to tell me everything, before he handed me the tapes and said he was so close to Fats now, we'd bust him like a balloon with the shit he knew, but he promised to talk to me later. Next think I knew the FBI called me in the sergeant's office."

Thaddeus cursed under his breath. "So you think Fats knows everything, including my involvement?"

"I really don't know. Pooh did have honest street connections. He probably received Fats trust by getting some of the women on that list. We don't know everything about all what is going on. I think he did it to save your ass. No one knows the connection between you and I and we're going to leave it like this, but I suggest you get a message through this girl and tell them you don't want her services anymore." They stepped off the elevator into a Laundromat room.

Thaddeus never expected to end it like this—so soon. He needed more time to evaluate his feelings more. He could not walk away now! "Now wait one moment. Are we abandoning the girl?"

"We've gotten all the information we need from her. We've had her tailed and identified as of two weeks ago. She knows absolutely nothing about her other life. She has hallucinations about being with you and can't figure out why, but her psychiatrist, who is in cahoots with Fats, just tells her they're dreams, which she readily believes. I think once we arrest everyone involved, she'll be left alone and chalk this one up as a strange experience in her life. Let her go Thaddeus. You'll never see her again and if you do and press the issue you might cause irreparable damage to her mental status."

Thaddeus couldn't let the Case go, not when he wanted to see her more. He was confused about his feelings for Skye and for the Case. With the realization closing in he was never going to see her again, how could he properly sort out his feelings for Skye. "I'm going to see her tonight. If not for her sanity, but for mine as well. She can't just forget about me. I know this sounds strange because you aren't there, but I feel it when she's with me she wants to be with me and I have a feeling if I don't end it properly, things won't be the same for . . . her." He almost said, "us."

Craig was having deep reservations about this. "Thad, I don't think that's a good idea."

"I'm doing it. You won't give me the information I want on her, then I'll continue to see her until I damn well please."

"Fine, I'll let you see her from afar, but that's it." He was adamant.

Thaddeus' cinnamon eyes danced with joy. "When?"

"Next week."

"Too long."

"I won't do it sooner. I don't think you can get involved with-"

Thaddeus cut him off, "I don't give a damn what you think, Craig, I want to see her, so I'll do it tonight and until she's out of my system. I'll find her on my own damn time and see her."

"Listen you selfish bastard, I won't let you harm her."

"You and what army plan to stop me?"

Craig could see he could not get Thaddeus to do as he wanted, so he compromised. "Alright, fine, see her tonight, but keep the microphone on and the panic button close near just in case, then Monday I will take you on a surveillance with me on her. She has a doctor's appointment scheduled and we want to see if she goes to it. We'll tail her from her home, but only if you swear tonight you finish this ridiculous obsession and promise you'll never step foot in her life again."

Thaddeus leaned against the wall to think. He wanted to protest, but the term selfish bastard hit hard in his conscious. He wasn't that selfish to cause irreparable damage to her. He would accept Craig's terms, but he wouldn't keep his word. This meant too much to him. "I won't if you do as you promised," he said.

Craig didn't trust a word he said, he shook on it. This was crazy and now he wished he had never gotten Thaddeus involved.

He pushed for the service elevator to come pickup Thaddeus. "You go back up alone. Meet me at the café about noon Monday. Go through the kitchen, to the back door and I'll be waiting for you outside of the loading dock by the grocery store."

The elevator doors opened and Thaddeus stepped in. "Can I just know her first name?"

"Thad!" he protested.

"Please Craig. As a blood brother, and friend, do this for me. I just want her first name. I'd just like to call her by; her first name for once."

Craig shook his head hopelessly, then sighed giving in. Just as the doors were about to close, he said the name, and missed the shock expression on Thaddeus' face.

When Thaddeus returned to his apartment, the words of Thomas' resounded loudly in his mind. "One and the same."

How could this be? Why didn't he realize it until now? What the hell should he do? Sitting down and carefully thinking about all of it, he began to put little by little together. The heavy make up hid everything from him. Whenever he had seen Skye, she usually kept her hair wrapped or pulled tightly back. When the woman he'd see on Saturday's kept her soft long curly hair loose. Skye always wore frumpy clothes and the woman he saw on Saturday's wore next to nothing.

The doorbell rung at ten-thirty exactly and he knew who it was. He dimmed all the lights and lit the fireplace. This time he didn't use the potion in her wine. He didn't pour the wine at all, wanting to do so after what he planned tonight

Slowly opening the door trying to control his eagerness to grab her in his arms and kiss her all over, his eyes noted every detail of her face and knew it was his Skye. Dressed in a flowing silk shoulder-less lavender gown that accentuated the color in her dancing eyes, she gave him the most radiating smile when he opened the door. Jasmine filled his nostrils as he pulled her in his arms, resisting the urge to kiss her, knowing if he did, he would lose what little control he possessed. His eyes needed more of the vision of loveliness he held.

She blushed. "I'm dreaming again, aren't I?" she asked.

"No," he whispered gruffly through his pent up passion.

Her arms circled his neck and her fingers caressed the nape. "No?" she asked amused. "I find it highly impossible to have *the* most gorgeous man looking at me like that."

"Like what?" he hungered to know.

"You want me. You want to make love to me. I can see it in those sensuous expressive eyes of yours, Thaddeus, but I want you to know exactly how much I want you too."

Her saying his name was his undoing. His lips melted together like hot molten lava. Her moist tongue entered his mouth and he accepted it willingly, voraciously needing her sweetness to fill him. Her hands moved down to his shirt and in her passionate haste she ripped the shirt opened. He didn't give her a chance to apologize as he yanked her away from the door while kicking it closed. Ripping the rest of the shirt off of him in one quick motion, he pulled her back in his arms and made an oral assault on her mouth that consumed her. Her fingers moved down to his pants and he helped her get past the belt and the zipper. It seemed choreographed as they moved around the room leaving a trail of clothes until they ended up on the rug in front of the fireplace where she finished undressing him. This was a unique experience for him. No woman had ever undressed him or been so dominant. He couldn't believe this was his Skye, yet he knew it was and couldn't stop her if he tried. Be damn his conscious, he wanted her with all his mind, body, and soul. He had resisted it because he was unsure of his feelings until now.

She pushed away suddenly from his kiss and held him at arms length. Even when he tried to yank her back, she resisted. "I need you as much as you need me right now, Thaddeus, but I intend to remember this night. It won't be pieces of a puzzle, it will be an entire dream from front to back." Her hands began to roam over his body slowly. "I want you to feel my wantonness, Thaddeus." What made this truly erotic was her lips followed the soft fingertips planting various kisses, licks, and nibbles all over his body. Before he could think of the trail she blazed all over his body, he felt himself being engulfed deeply into her oral cavity. His legs swayed unsteadily and she placed a hand on his thigh as if to hold him. She took him to the edge of orgasm, but ceased his flow just as he was about to release. Her hands massaged, stroked, and fondled so affectionately, he cried out her name several times begging for release. She guided him down to his knees until they were eye to eye.

Cupping his face, steering his eyes to meet hers, she smiled seeing the want in his eyes. "I want you as much as you want me, Thaddeus. Did I make you feel it?"

He nodded.

"Know this is how I will always feel for you. Remember it." She lightly kissed his brow, then his two eyelids.

He was speechless. This was a dream come true for him. Knowing she wanted him this much threw whatever sense of morality out the window. He gently pulled the straps off her shoulders and laid her down under him on the soft rug in front of the fire. The kiss he bestowed upon her now, was filled with gentleness and understanding. She wanted this night to be remembered and he would acquiesce to her needs and desires despite his own thirst to take her. Their tongues explored one another with deep realization that this was not just sex, but lovemaking on a level higher than the world around them.

Entering her was pure heaven, and bringing her to pleasure with him, was a pinnacle of enjoyment. She held him so closely and gently bit down on his shoulder near a burn scar in the shape of a strawberry below his collarbone. She didn't know why this was so significant, as her tongue traced the shape around the edges of the scar.

He sighed in pleasure turning his lips to her ear. "You are wonderful, Skye."

She giggled knowingly. "You aren't so bad yourself."

Thaddeus smiled knowing this was the real Skye speaking. She was accepting the dream as it was: just a dream. He whispered, remembering the microphone was on. "If this was real would you still have me as a friend?"

She shook her head and as if knowing he wanted this only for her ears, whispered back, "I would have you as a lover."

"And if you knew in reality I wanted you as much as I have shown in this dream what would you do?"

She paused a little hesitant, then whispered back, "Cry, cause I wouldn't know what to do with you."

He chuckled deeply and she gasped feeling vibrating tingles in her belly. He was still embedded to the hilt in her and unquestionable firm even though he spent himself, but his body was still aroused from their joining and 'pillow talk.' "You could just love me."

"Ah, but would you love someone as plain as me this much forever?" She asked not really expecting an answer.

He moved up until he could look in her eyes. "You are not plain Skye. You are the most extraordinary woman I have ever met. Yes, I could love you much more."

Skye smiled not expecting that answer, but adoring the answer she had received. She pulled him down to kiss him briefly, then smiled wickedly. "Show me again and maybe I will believe it when I wake up alone in my bed."

That was all the encouragement he needed, to begin another round of lovemaking that lasted until the early morning.

Chapter 18

Skye wasn't sure but she swore she was still in his arms. She couldn't be absolutely sure, yet she didn't want to open her eyes to disappointment. Taking a check on all her body parts, she realized she was naked under the covers. She never slept naked! She also realized if she didn't make love last night, then why did every muscle in her body hurt like hell.

Finally she lifted her eyelids to disappointment. She was in her room, in her bed, alone. "Show me again and maybe I will believe it when I wake up alone in my bed." Those words rang aloud in her head like a bell.

Sitting up, her body gasped as memories flooded. She remembered! She remembered so vividly, she could have passed out from embarrassment. The only thing confusing her was, even though she remembered calling his name, she couldn't remember his face. It was a blur. Even when she fudged through breakfast racking her mind over it, she couldn't really come up with a definite picture in her mind. Was it a dream or reality? If it was a dream, why was she feeling it now, and if it was reality, why couldn't she remember the details?

It made no sense and she would go crazy if she racked her brain anymore. Taking a long shower, she decided to go to the grocery store to take her mind off of it all. Plus, she needed some fresh air. Before leaving she went over to the fax machine, because she heard it go off. It was from John Dandridge. Eager to know what he was talking about, yet wanting to hurry and get out the door, she decided to stick the fax in her back pants pocket and read it while at the grocery store.

Before leaving out the house, she found an old army knife with a belt and wrapped it around her ankle using her loose pants to cover this up. If she was going in public she wanted to make sure she had a weapon of some kind.

As she parked in the parking lot at the shopping strip where she had first met Thaddeus Newman, she convinced herself it was a dream. Talking to Thaddeus these past two days had just made her hallucinations stronger to the point that her mind was affecting her body. It would be impossible for her to have made love to him because she was certain they had not made love at her home. The place she'd dreamed of was much too expensive, and she had not driven her car last night, because the odometer was in the same place she had left it yesterday. Although there was the question of her pajamas being at the foot of her bed, she could have easily kicked them off since the dream was so intense. Maybe her period was coming, she concluded. Her body always acted strange when her period came on, although the birth control had immediately began to work on cutting down her flow.

So if Thaddeus called her today? She would just pretend like the hallucination never happened. It never happened so why should she feel embarrassed about it. She would act normal when she spoke to him, but she would let him know of the medical center. He might know someone privately on the police force that could assist her. When she thought about just walking into a police station, she thought about the articles she had found in the library about two cops beating a witness who was part of Trevor Coleman's case the police were forming against the crime boss. The cops mysteriously received five thousand dollars that could not be traced to any one or any business. Internal Affairs suspected the money had come from 'an illegal source.' She did not want to be beaten half to death and left in a coma for the rest of her life, which is what happened to the victim. Regular cops could not be trusted when it came to Trevor Coleman.

Getting out the car, and grabbing a buggy, she went inside the grocery store for an uneventful time.

Going to the vegetable aisle first, she picked out a nice cantaloupe. There was a specialty oil rack nearby and for some reason she was drawn to it. Not only did it have cooking oils, but potpourri oils as well. Her fingers clearly weeded out all other bottles and went straight for what her senses were picking up on.

Pulling the bottle off the shelf, she immediately drew it to her nose and closed her eyes.

Behind her a deep voice said near her ear, "jasmine."

Warm shivers went down her spine, and then she opened her eyes telling herself she was not hallucinating. Turning around abruptly, her eyes went wide as she met those beautiful dancing cinnamon eyes and jumped back from his propinquity. In her haste she knocked over the specialty rack and a table of onions that were behind the rack. She stumbled back and fell hard on her butt under more onions.

Skye was embarrassed beyond belief and buried her face in her hands not believing the reality that was happening at this moment. Others gathered around her, but all she could hear was her heartbeat pounding in her ears.

Closing her eyes tightly she forced herself to take control of her emotions and not act like a ninny around him. His attention was still new to her and she wondered would she ever get use to this man and what he did to her equilibrium.

Composing herself, she took a deep breath and put her hands down. A clerk asked her if she was all right and she nodded. Thaddeus still stood above her looking quite concerned. Of course he was, she had just behaved like a ninny. Skye told herself she must get over her nervousness around him.

"May I help you up?" the clerk asked.

"I'll do it," Thaddeus growled giving the clerk a red heated glare of jealousy.

The clerk saw the intensity in his eyes and backed away.

Thaddeus outstretched his hand to her and she took it hoping her palms didn't sweat as he gently pulled her up. She almost slipped again on an onion, but he used his other arm to quickly come around her and steady her against him. Their bodies were pressed against each other and she looked up into his eyes. He was searching for something with his eyes. What? She quickly lowered her eyes to his neck, and when she still felt uncomfortable, her eyes lowered to his partially opened shirt where she was looking directly at his collarbone.

Her breathing stopped and her mouth dropped open. She wanted to scream, she wanted to faint, she wanted to shake, but her body nor mind would not move or respond to anything she wanted to do. Instead her hands gripped his arms harder until her nails dug in his skin, but he didn't seem to notice. He was still watching her.

Her eyes would not let go of the strawberry shaped burn scar under his collarbone. She wrenched her hands free from his arms and moved it up to his shirt. Before he could stop her she tore open the shirt revealing the think brawny chest. The crowd that had gathered around them, gasped, but Thaddeus didn't move as her eyes slowly engulfed the scar then slowly moved over to his shoulder, where he still bore the love bite she had put on him last night.

Tears of realization filled those beautiful lavender eyes, as they slowly moved up his neck, over his tight lips, his flaring nose and to those expressive eyes. Eyes that told her what they had shared was the truth. *All if it!*

'It was no dream!' her mind screamed.

With all the strength, confusion, and disgust inside of her, she bawled her fist up and connected it to his face. The crowd gasped louder.

He still didn't move or respond.

"YOU . . . STAY AWAY . . . F-FROM ME!" she screamed backing away sobbing with every word, gasping for every breath. The blackness tried to engulf her, but she shook it away, grasping at her inner strength, pushing her consciousness to not give in to the panic attack that was blanketing her being.

He could see she was fighting herself not to fall to pieces. Damn, what had he done? Damn, Damn, his selfishness. Thaddeus tried to repair the damage and explain. "I didn't know it was you until last night. I didn't know for sure until you showed up at the door." He tried to grab her, but she jerked away.

"DON'T TOUCH ME," she seethed through clenched teeth. There were too many emotions grabbling inside of her making it difficult to speak, to think, to breathe.

"Please don't do this," he begged. "I thought-" He couldn't finish because the tears from her eyes flowed too heavily. This was affecting her more than he thought. He hadn't thought this through carefully. Damn, Damn, Damn!

Gathering her strength like a robe to enshroud her soul, she ran out the store not stopping until she reached her car.

He followed her, but she had pulled off before he reached the little black Escort. He cared little about anything else. Her mind was not stable and he needed to make sure. Calling Craig he admitted everything. He even admitted being a selfish bastard. "I don't care what you have to do, we have to find her. She looked ready to crack. Please Craig, help me."

"I'll see what I can do. What time does your flight leave?"

"Fuck that! I won't leave until I know she is all right. Come get me." He would just call Thomas to let him know to go to Chicago without him to meet Detective Heart about the daughter.

"I'll be there in an hour and we'll go by her place."

*   *   *

When she arrived home, she almost turned into the driveway, but saw the front door opened and pulled away slowly not attracting attention to her car. Going to a nearby party store she pulled her car into the parking lot. Walking around the block down the alley-way, she went back to her house from behind. Peering over the fence of her backyard, she recognized Alan and Dr. Ryan Carter standing on the back porch having a cigarette. They were in deep frustrated discussion.

". . . should haven taken the drug away from them then, Rye and not waited for them to find out so much. How the hell could you not know they've been out the country since yesterday? I told you to keep tabs on them. They probably told her everything."

"If they told her everything, she would have been at the nearest police station last night not up at the River Place with Newman. She probably doesn't realize a damn thing. I find her very naïve and readily acceptable to the situation. That's why she was the perfect candidate," Dr. Carter defended himself.

"Naïve? That bitch has got evidence that connects us to the center." He shook a hand full of papers. "All my pop needs to know is that you let her go and you're toast Ryan. You're gonna end up just like your partners—dead."

Other noises could be heard from inside the house, and Alan angrily called in from the back door, "Stop making all that fucking noise for the police come."

She ducked down the alley again and waited in an unknown backyard storage shed until nightfall. Waiting gave her time to sort out her thoughts and feelings about Thaddeus Newman. As she relaxed and concentrated more, her thoughts made the strawberry shaped scar more evident in her mind and what she had done last night. The love they made had not been given from a man with lustful intentions and as she remembered how wanton she had behaved the end results was bound to happen, yet he still could have stopped her. He must have known she wasn't in her right mind. 'He must have!' she repeatedly tried to convince herself.

Feeling herself becoming frustrated about this matter, she turned her thoughts to how she had gotten in this situation. She had always been a person who didn't trust anyone, so how had she allowed this drug to come into her life.

The only way she could reason everything was that, Dr. Himes was a doctor. She had always been close to Dr. Welch and moving to the big city all alone away from Dr. Welch had probably shifted her trust over to these doctors. These doctors weren't really there to help people, but to hurt them, caring not whom they killed to get their stupid research to work.

When the coast was clear at her home and all was quiet, she

jumped over the fence going straight to the doghouse. Dr. Carter and Alan now knew how much information on them she knew and she didn't want to die. Now the police needed to know and she needed to enlist the help of the only person she trusted at this moment—Thaddeus.

As she was about to leave out the yard, several police cars pulled up and a detective car came all the way in the driveway. She ducked down behind the doghouse and watched. The driver got out saying, "Stay in here, Thad. I want to check the house one more time. This might not be good." He walked in the house. Soon as the other policemen followed, she gasped as Thaddeus got out the car. How did he get involved so soon?

Thaddeus, being stubborn as a bull, went into the house as well. Soon as the coast was clear she hopped back over the fence and went around a neighbor's house while they were all inside. There was one cop on the porch waiting, but not looking her way. She checked to see if the back of the detective car was unlocked. To her blessing, the handle went all the way up and she crawled inside with her bag and ducked down.

After fifteen minutes, both men sat in front.

"Dammit Thaddeus this would have never happened if you had listened to me. You knew getting near her would do this."

"Don't you think I don't know that now? Don't think I'm not cursing myself."

"Don't think! Don't think or talk anymore. You've done quite enough."

It was quiet as Craig swerved the car sharply around a corner. In the silence, she sat calmly in the middle of the backseat.

"HOLY SHIT!" Craig screamed swerving suddenly to the side of the road.

"What's wrong?" Thaddeus asked looking back in the direction of Craig's eyes. "Holy shit!"

Craig looked around at her. "Where the hell have you been?" he demanded to know.

"Skye . . ." Thaddeus begin.

"Don't talk to me. Don't say one word to me," she sneered at Thaddeus. "I never want to speak to you again." Both of the men could hear the wavering of her voice on the brink of insanity.

Thaddeus forgot reason and started to speak again.

"I will throw you out of this car, if you keep being selfish, Thaddeus. You even admitted when you wanted me to find her you were a selfish bastard," Craig threatened. "She has been through enough of your shit so don't say one more fucking word or I'll make sure you can't see straight. Dammit, I should have pulled you from undercover when I knew you were too emotionally involved."

Thaddeus gave her one last look. It was too dark to see her facial expression, but he could just imagine. Ominous and expressionless. He briskly turned around deciding he could ignore the both of them.

Craig took off again. "Ms Patterson, I'm taking you down to the precinct."

"It will be too late. We have to go the medical center. They know how much I know about the drugs and women and the list."

He looked in the rearview mirror. "What list?"

"The list with all the women names on it. They are going to recruit them so they can use them, just like they used m-me." Her voice faltered a little.

Thaddeus almost spoke again, but bit his lip fighting for control wanting grievously to attest he had not meant to use her. Yet the though of her losing what little hold on reality she had, and Craig threatening to punch his lights out made him halt the urge. "Alan had the list at the party. I made a copy of it. I have it in my bag."

"You have a copy? What else do you have?"

"We have to hurry," she admonished. "They know I know."

He changed directions and begin driving towards the medical center. "How much do you know?"

"Everything," she exasperated. "The drug is a birth control hallucinogenic mind controlling substance. They are somehow able to control me using some device—a phone ringing, clapping of hands, an alarm . . . so I can do whatever they want me to do. I heard them talking. They said they had to many dangerous investors who would not be happy if they didn't do what they were supposed to do. I know they used GHB in their product which is illegal in the state of Michigan."

Craig began to call back up as she continued.

"I pretended to be passed out. I didn't know the seriousness of it until this afternoon when I learned that the other doctors were killed."

"You know this for sure?"

"I heard Alan saying so this afternoon when I returned home and saw them ransacking my place."

He stopped at the center. There were cops and swat already there. "Stay here," he ordered both of them. "Keep your mouth shut," he specifically ordered Thaddeus who was still pouting about the remark Craig made earlier.

Craig got out leaving them alone. At first she was afraid, but then she became concerned about what the officer in charge of the medical center scene was telling Craig about the area.

"They're all gone," she said reading the officers lips. "They moved everything because they know I know, but they aren't far." Images danced in her head as her mind was prodding her memory to release the information her subconscious wanted to hold on to. Miraculously despite the stress she was under, her brain began to allow flashes of pictures, places . . . a warehouse near the waterfront. She knew exactly where it was. Time was running out and they would know if the police knew because the beady eyed man had some of the cops in his back pocket.

Thaddeus wanted to turn around, but he didn't want her to go into hysterics again.

"We have to hurry." Her vision spotted the keys in the ignition and Skye knew what she had to do. She pushed the bag to the side and crawled into the front seat. He watched as she looked around, then cranked the car up. Craig didn't hear the ignition come to life, but when the car went into reverse smashing against another patrol car; he started running for the car ordering her to stop and for Thaddeus to stop her. The car jerked into drive gruffly. Putting her foot hard down on the pedal, the engine was reborn. Thaddeus allowed her to drive for about five minutes without saying a word, and then decided to ask her their destination in a nonchalant manner.

"The warehouses. Didn't he tell you to shut your mouth?" she snapped.

He shut his mouth again concluding she had lost her mind and when Craig caught up with them Thaddeus would not be the blame for her insanity this time.

Pulling up to a downtown wharf and parking, she looked around as she got out the car. He followed her meeting her in the front of the car. Closing her eyes she tried to remember the strange ringing of the phone from last night. She had gotten up and went downstairs in her house, then unlocked her door and went right back to sleep. When she awoke again, she was in a limousine with white lining. A deep voice was talking while an oriental woman was combing her hair. They pulled right into this warehouse and . . .

She relaxed herself and stood straight up, pretending to get out the car. The oriental woman guided her around the car and down the wharf behind one of the warehouses to a back entrance.

Thaddeus watched as she began to go down the wharf towards the third warehouse, but instead of going in the front of them, she ducked behind them. He caught up, but she suddenly disappeared in front of him. Out of nowhere, a sharp object knocked him on the side of his head and darkness surrounded him.

Alan stepped out of the darkness and looked accusingly over at Dr. Carter, who looked confused. "I thought you said she wouldn't remember."

"Her personality clearly shows she is not one to take charge."

"Fuck that science bullshit! That's probably what she wanted you to think."

Dr. Carter was quiet until he recognized the face of the man. "What is she doing with him?"

"Shouldn't I be asking you, doctor?" Alan seethed. He turned to the ominous figure behind him. "Help him get them inside, then get rid of that car. I don't want more to come." He went inside where the temporary setup was moved.

Fats stood up from his desk on the platform. "What the hell is going on out there?"

"Dr. Carter was wrong about the girl. She is starting to remember."

"How? The others never remembered."

"That's because the others were already into their second or third injection before they realized their minds were deteriorating." Alan cursed angrily. "We've got to get out of here tonight, not tomorrow."

"Did she come alone?"

"No, matter of fact, she brought Newman with her. Don't ask me how that happened."

Trisha stood up from behind Fats and Alan knew immediately the answer to his question. He came stomping around the desk. "You did this didn't you?" he raged grabbing her shoulders and digging his fingers in her skin.

She cried in pain, shaking her head. "No, I didn't I swear. I didn't do anything, Trevor."

"Let her go," Fats said disgustedly. "Just start packing up." He gathered his bag. "Have Butts to watch them while you get all this shit destroyed. Those two can die in the fire with the rest of them. Take care of the doctor yourself, and get yourself and Trisha out the city. I'm taking the train out tonight and we'll meet in Chatham over in Canada tomorrow afternoon."

Alan watched as his father left out. He turned again to Trisha who cowered at the vicious look in his beady black eyes. "I'll take care of you later."

"Y-You aren't going to kill them in the fire are you?" she asked.

"None of your business." He threw the keys at her. "Get the hell out of here."

She scrambled for the keys and hurried out the warehouse,

but she didn't go to the car. Instead she looked up at the fire escape, which led to the top loft of the warehouse. Tucking the keys in her pants she started quietly climbing the fire escape.

*   *   *

Opening her eyes slowly, she could hear Dr. Carter's voice, ". . . destroy my work? No Alan, I will not destroy everything I have done. You must be crazy. This is the best scientific breakthrough and you just expect me to throw it away. Burn all this work? Now that those old farts are out the picture, the profit and rights solely belong to me. You'd be destroying millions of dollars."

She moved her head slightly, then gasped. She was leaning against someone warm, with very broad shoulders.

"Are you speaking to me now?" Thaddeus asked quietly.

"I wasn't awake to say no, but now that I am, no I'm not speaking to you."

He could hear the sarcasms in her tone and ignored it. "The huge man just left out when Alan came in to tell him something. I know it's him, even though I'm blindfolded. I recognized his voice."

"Do you think Trisha is involved?" she asked.

"I don't know. I haven't heard her or heard Alan mention her. Can you wiggle out the ropes?"

She tried, but it was extremely difficult. "I don't think I can, but I can reach your hands and untie your ropes." Skye began to do so despite the ropes digging at her back and chest.

The ropes popped from around his wrist. He quickly untied himself, then turned toward her and began to unwrap her. Both of them heard the loud footsteps and he began to go even faster. They knew someone was coming.

He released her quickly and ducked behind the door. The ominous figure entered and she drew his attention when she gasped at the size of him then gasped at how horribly scarred his face was. Thaddeus had grabbed a steel chair and slammed it across his back. The seven-foot ugly giant fell to the floor at her feet. She looked up at Thaddeus. "Did you kill him?"

"I was trying."

She shuddered. The man had been horrendous looking. A long face that bared deep scars as if someone had tried to slash him to death with a hot knife. With his added size was just as apparitional. Skye stood and quickly stretched while Thaddeus peeked out the door to see if they had warranted company or if someone was coming. He glanced back at her to see her looking about the room. Her bag was over in a corner and she reached in there to look around.

"My proof is still here. They didn't check the bag."

He looked around the room to see a fire escape near the ceiling. If they crawled over on the wooden crates, they could make it. She followed his directions and went over to it already reading his mind. With his assistance she allowed him to help her up giving him a very wary look as if any touch from him would drive her crazy. While she did this, he went over to Butts and grabbed the rope they had been tied with. Hurrying up, he started to tie the giant's hands, but just as he was finished Butts awoke and grabbed Thad's wrist in a vicious vise that was unbreakable. Thaddeus tried with all his might to pull away, but it was impossible. The man had super human strength. In his struggle he looked up to see Skye was almost at the top. Butts yanked Thaddeus around, and then practically threw him against the wall knocking the breath out of him. This gave Butts a chance to break the ropes around his wrist and head for Skye.

Skye saw how the giant had thrown Thaddeus around like a rag doll and she knew if the monster got his hands on her, she'd be like paper in his hands. Climbing faster, she saw the man coming to the boxes. Just as she was about to reach the top and grab a hold to the windowsill, it opened. At the same time, the boxes begin to sway, then fall. She grabbed the sill in time and looked up as she dangled from her hold.

"Skye, grab my arm!" Trisha ordered reaching down trying to pull her up.

Skye knew she had no choice but to let her help. Climbing out the window, she looked back to see Thaddeus wrestling with man. He was getting the crap kicked out of him. She screamed as the giant slammed a powerful fist into Thad's stomach, and when Thaddeus hurled over in pain, the giant's colossal knee came up and knocked him on his back. Trisha pulled her away from the opening.

"We can't save him. We've got to go," she admonished.

"They're going to kill him!" she cried.

"They won't. We can get to the police in time. He's too valuable."

She reasoned she could. Craig had to know where they were by now. Following Trisha to the fire escape, she almost bumped into the woman's back as Trisha stopped and began to back up. Skye looked past Trisha to see five men with guns pointing at them. Skye would admit right now, she was not having a good day.

Chapter 19

Cold water awakened him. He had been in excruciating pain when he passed out and returning to consciousness hurt like hell. "Come on Thad, you're gonna miss the fun," Alan's voice cajoled him awake.

"You can't do this, Alan!" he heard Trisha screamed.

A slap and scream made him open his eyes. "Skye," he growled.

Alan turned around from Trisha cowed body on the floor. Two men grabbed her and dragged her to a chair next to Skye who was tied down with her arms straight out in front of her. Her mouth was covered. Amazingly, her demeanor was rather calm. He wondered would he ever see her with an expression like he saw her just that morning. He could have made love to her then if he didn't think she would lose what little sanity the drug had left her. He wondered if he would ever make love to her again?

Skye's eyes suddenly widened with understanding. She could read his thoughts and was mortified he was thinking about that right now. She avoided his eyes on purpose cursing her own self for being concerned about him.

Trisha started protesting about being tied up. Dr. Carter came in the room. They were back where they started. The boxes were moved around to give them more room. There were two extra Debo-looking guards strapped with semi-automated weapons in hand standing next to him and the other next to Trisha holding her as if she could just jump from the bindings that held her tightly in the chair. Skye could see propane tanks and methane fuel drums around them. The room smelled like it had been newly painted, but Skye suspected there must be a large shipment of paint thinner somewhere because it was one of the main contents of GHB. Skye had to get out of this—alive—hopefully with Thaddeus if not anything else. Her brain began to think of a solution to their problem amazingly working quite well under pressure. She loved a deadline.

"I have worked damn hard to get this drug invented. What pimp wouldn't want his hands on this?" Alan went over to the tray Dr. Carter had brought in. "If the American government won't approve of it, then maybe my friends in the underground will support me in my effort to give women more freedom. I have made it possible for the Middle-American woman to explore what her soul really wants. Sexual freedom."

"You'll never get away with this, Alan. There are too many connections to your father that lead to you. You'll be caught and put away." Thaddeus decided to buy time by talking out everything. Hopefully Craig was on his way and would save them somehow. He tried his bonds but he figured that big oaf of a killer would have double tied everything to make sure they wouldn't get out this time. He knew Skye must be in pain as tight as her ropes looked. He surveyed the room as much as he could. There were three men, plus Laroche, Dr. Carter and Alan present in the room.

Before Alan began speaking to them again, he told one of the guards to gather everyone up and get the supplies down to the boats, because he would be joining them shortly. "I will get away with it, because with the vials we've collected I have done what these doctors and street pharmacists have only dreamed of. You or your stupid cop friends won't be able to stop me."

Thaddeus snorted. It sounded so cliché—ick. "So you intend to kill me, get away with the money and the supplies, then live happily ever after in South America or some beach in Jamaica?"

"Oh no. I'm gong to inject you with our drug. It won't do what it does to women. It has a counter effect. The large dose of estrogen takes away the sexual drive of man, and instead of going unconscious to get hallucinations, you'll be wide awake and see things like you've never seen before. It's the perfect high, Thaddeus. You will go slowly insane and soon you won't be able to function like a normal human being. You will slowly go crazy and no one can stop it. No one! In men, the drug does not have to be injected into you several times; It reacts to the testosterone levels in your system and produce the exact same drug increasing naturally as the synthetic form decreases. No one will know what is wrong with you, as your body and mind grow weak and soon you will perish from mental health and no one will be the wiser. It will affect you instantly so by the time the police arrive, you'll be too out of your mind to do anything." He laughed wickedly.

Dr. Carter prepared three needles to be used and set them on a small table near Skye's chair, right by her arm.

"You have three needles. What do you intend to do with the other two?"

Alan turned towards Skye and Trisha. "Although Ms Patterson has been useful in our experiments, Thaddeus, she had become a bad investments. She knows too much and that is not good." He leaned his face inches from Skye's eyes. "Didn't anyone ever tell you ignorance is bliss, Ms Patterson?"

Her eyes slanted to slits. "Did anyone tell you brushing twice a day fights halitosis?" she sneered viciously.

He backhanded her. Skye's head swung back, but came forward. Trisha screamed for her, but Skye didn't cry. "She also mentioned you hit like a bitch." The second backhand against the other side of her face made her see double. He would have delivered another, but Dr. Carter stopped him by grabbing his wrist.

"She'll get hers when we kill her with the overdose."

Alan cursed under his breath giving Skye a vicious look. "I'm going to take pleasure in watching you die, but I want you to see how you're going to die first." He went over to Trisha and held her head back. Trisha pleaded with Alan for her life.

"Why don't you tell them Trisha? Tell them how you begged me to accept Mr. Newman and find him a really nice girl. Boy weren't you surprised to see them working together. It was all fault they are in this mess, but that is fine. Seeing you die will pleasure me in a way you have never done." His face was mere centimeters

from her. She screamed as the needle was pushed into her arm, but
he didn't pump the chemical inside of her yet.

Skye remained calm and steadily worked at the rope. She was
halfway through. Alan had his back to her and the tray with two
more needles filled with the chemical sat right next to her arm. If
she could just unthread a little faster everything would be fine.

"Alan, please," Trisha begged. "I'm going to be your wife."

"You were my sweet." He kissed her forehead and Trisha let out
the most gut wrenching blood-curdling scream Skye had ever heard
from anyone making the hair on the back of her neck stand up.

Thaddeus watched as her body went limp when the liquid in
the vial disappeared into her arm. Trisha's whole body began to
jostle in painful spasms. Alan went over to Skye who had her face
turned away. "Watch," he sneered holding her head stiff so she
could watch as Trisha's body reacted violently to the high dose of
chemical given to her. "Yours will be even worse you know," he
jeered in a whisper near her ear.

As he talked, she used this time to go even faster pretending
her movements were of struggling. She was quarter of a way done.
Trisha was trying to fight. Her words gurgled in her throat as the
sporadic moments became demoniac moments of pain and tor-
ture. Skye wanted to screams, to cry, to save Trisha from the awful
distress. It was too late. There was no antidote. Once taken in that
amount, there would not be anything to save anyone.

Trisha suddenly stopped convulsing sporadically and her wide
big brown doe eyes met Skye's. "F-Freeee . . . y-yaaa—soooff,"
she forcefully gurgled out, then her body began again more de-
monic spasms as thick white saliva shot out her throat and nose.
Everyone, except Skye was engrossed at the death dance Trisha's
body elicited. The room seemed mesmerized as Trisha fought to
stay alive, screaming incoherently. Skye knew Trisha was holding
on for her sake. Trisha must have known Skye was trying to become free.

At that moment, just when Skye knew Trisha could not fight
it anymore, the last thread flicked away. Alan was engrossed in

watching his fiancée die. The rope fell away from her arm and Skye knew her plan of action.

Thaddeus' peripheral vision saw the rope fall from Skye's wrist. It was slow motion from then on as she wrenched from Alan's grasp. The man was so shocked he couldn't stop her and before he alerted anyone she grabbed the syringes off the table next to her and jabbed one in his eye. Thaddeus saw the liquid vomit into his face from the needlepoint. A second later, Skye had attained a knife out of her sock and freed her other wrist. She flicked the knife to the floor at Thad's feet as Dr. Carter came for her. With the second syringe in her left hand, she swiftly fought away his arms that tried to grab her with her right hand, and jabbed the long needle in his neck, but she didn't release it. Dr. Carter froze instantly a look of terror filled his eyes.

Thaddeus used this opportunity to grab the knife with his feet and bring it up until his hands could grab it.

The other guard and the ugly giant looked at her amazed at her speed.

"Don't come any close or the only doc left who can make your drug will be gone."

The giant tried her by stepping a little forward.

Carter felt the needle turn a little. "Dammit do as she says!" he hissed deathly afraid to move. He looked over at Alan, whose body was convulsing on the floor.

She moved to get comfortable, never letting go the needle in his neck. Bending him back into her, with her body behind him, she was able to look at the entire room. "You didn't tell the others why the drugs make woman go crazy, did you, Carter?" she asked him.

"I-I don't know what you mean," he pretended not to know nervously.

"It slowly eats away the myelin in the brain; the only protection which guards the nerves from being exposed. You didn't tell them, because you knew what it would do. Didn't you? So you had them killed because either one of them found out, or they already knew too much."

"I killed them for what they knew. H-How did you find out about the myelin?"

"I had samples broken down. One of the chemicals used is a substance that eats feeds on the protein the myelin has, but controls the subconscious. You planned on taking over the world like that, Carter?"

"I had big plans for the drug, you'll destroy it all if you kill me. I could help people with brain injuries become new people. Permanent identity losses could be regenerated. I could use it to tap in the human subconscious and open tremendous possibilities for the neurology community.

"Instead you decide to use it on unsuspecting woman for a two bit pimp!" she sneered. "I should kill you just for that."

He cried out feeling the needle pressing into his skin more. "The greater good! It was all for the greater good."

Suddenly the door opened and Craig burst in. Thaddeus jumped up from the chair and at the same time, the giant used the distraction of the door opening to grab his gun out his jacket and aim it at Skye. Thaddeus lunged for Laroche's brawny arm, throwing his weight against the man. The gun went off and the second gunman went down who was just about to aim for Craig.

"Freeze!" Craig yelled.

In the same instant, Skye became diverted by the action and Carter used this opportunity to grab her wrist pulling the needle out his neck then shoved her against the wall.

Craig pressed the gun against Dr. Carter's temple. "I said freeze asshole."

The gun Thaddeus and Laroche were wrestling for went off again. This bullet went straight through Craig's right shoulder throwing him against the door. Dr. Carter ran out the room. Skye who'd been a bit shaken got up and ran after Dr. Carter. Laroche threw Thaddeus off of him and barreled out the room after Skye.

Thaddeus ran to Craig to see how seriously hurt he was. Craig screeched as Thaddeus shook him. He pressed his gun in Thaddeus hand. "Go after her. She's going to get herself killed." He pulled out a walkie-talkie for backup and medic to come right away.

Thaddeus ran out the door and down the stairs. He could hear footsteps below him and figured they were heading to the lower levels. Following their path would take forever. He had to beat them to the lower levels before they got there. He spotted a pole that secured the rails connecting each level together and jumped up to the steel pole. Sliding carefully down to the second level, then to the first where Dr. Carter was just arriving at the bottom of the steps. He was looking behind him to see where Skye was so he didn't see when Thaddeus jumped in front of him. Once he turned his head, Thaddeus took the butte of the gun and drove it into Dr. Carter's forehead. The man flew back almost knocking Skye down. Thaddeus, stepping by Dr. Carter's head, grabbed her behind him, then aimed the gun at the steps as the giant started to burrow down. "Get out of here," he ordered her then shot over Laroche's head, which made the Goliath instantly stop on the middle of the steps and hold up the gun as if to surrender. Yet his eyes were filled with hate and . . . death.

Skye started running out the building, but halted near the large cargo doors to see what happened.

"Throw the gun down here," Thaddeus ordered.

Instead of throwing the weapon down to Thaddeus' feet, he tossed it about six feet to the right near some cargo boxes that read: DANGER! HARZARDOUS CHEMICALS. In a menacing voice that sounded like a thick deep chain rattling, he said, "You'll never live to see another day."

"You are the one who won't be living, you sick fuck, now get down here slowly—" Thaddeus was grabbed from the back of his leg by the doctor and pushed off balance. He fell back as his gun was flung out of his hands from his fall. He kicked at the side of Dr. Carter's temple and instantly knocked the doctor out again, but the giant came running down the steps grabbing Thaddeus by his collar.

Thaddeus was lifted two feet off the ground trying to swing his legs to do some bodily damage to the Goliath's legs. Laroche's meaty fist jammed into his jaw sending Thaddeus sprawling to the floor. He got up—dazed—on the defense, but not sure which way was up.

Laroche smiled almost amazed at this young man's stamina. This one was big, but Laroche was larger, yet he felt he hadn't had a good physical challenge in a long while. Killing the fresh buck with his bare hands would give him great pleasure.

Skye watched as Thaddeus ducked from those huge swings Laroche delivered and whenever the defenses were down, Thaddeus got a good punch into the chest or face. He was quick and hit hard whenever he got a chance, but she knew if Laroche got in just a couple of hits, Thaddeus wouldn't see the light of day again. Searching the floor, she noted the gun near their fighting and decided to run for it.

Thaddeus saw her, and this distracted him. Those stone fist of Laroche came horribly down on his chest almost knocking the breathe out of him again. This gave Laroche time to run for the gun, which was Skye's aim as well. She picked the weapon up first and aimed the .38 at him, but the first shot went right past his ear to a small barrel of paint thinner that exploded instantly upon impact across the warehouse floor. There wasn't a lot of flammable liquid inside the barrel because the blast didn't scatter a lot of debris. Before she could get another shot off, he grabbed her around her waist and lifted her against him almost squeezing the wind from her body making her drop the gun to the floor. She gasped for air, then curled her head down and clamped her teeth into his arm, at the same time lifting her ankle and hitting his groin with the heel of her shoes. He dropped from the severe pain letting her go as well, but then saw his mistake and tried to reach for her again while standing up. With all his might, Thaddeus charged for Laroche and tackled him in the stomach. Laroche feeling himself losing balance grabbed Thaddeus jacket and they fell down together near the liquid flames burning all around them. Thaddeus situated himself in the upper position on top of Laroche somehow getting his arms pinned underneath his knees and began to swing like mad at his face.

Skye saw the liquid coming towards Thaddeus and Laroche. Running to Thaddeus, she grabbed him by the collar and pulled him away just as the liquid touched Laroche's pants leg. The flames followed only a second later and Laroche was engulfed in flames in minutes. He began to scream in pain as the fire enveloped him from head to toe.

Skye ran for a fire extinguisher as Thaddeus took his jacket off to try to get Laroche to roll the fire out. He took the extinguisher away and told her to get back as he aimed it toward Laroche. She could hear the sirens in the background as Thaddeus put the fire out on Laroche, but it was too late.

Skye went behind Thaddeus and circled her arms around his chest. He turned to face her holding close burying his face in the crook of her neck. "He's dead. He can't hurt us anymore," she assured him rubbing his back for comfort.

He looked over at Dr. Carter who was still passed out. "I guess it is."

A sense of elation filled her and she began to cry.

Thaddeus held her closer, but he didn't relax until he felt her body lean into his. Now would be the time to make everything up to her. Yes, he had done a great wrong to her. One he was very sorry for, but on the other hand, he could not feel sorry for doing it. Making love to her had been the greatest experience ever and he would have done it all over again given the chance. Yet, he wanted more than just her body, or her consent, which she had not given freely. He wanted to posses all of her with her willingly.

Chapter 20

Moving back in her house escorted by the police, had not been that difficult. For three months she had been holed up inside of a hotel room, until Cole Forsythe was caught crossing the Wisconsin/Canadian border and charged with murder, money laundering, illegal drug trade—including prosecution involving possession, manufacture and selling of GHB—prostitution, and attempted murder against seventeen young women, including Skye who testified. He and his major cohorts would serve for lifetimes to come without the chance of parole.

Somehow Alan Coleman had survived the assault from her and was convicted of a life sentence, but he was also suffering from GHB withdrawal in the Wayne County Jail. He was having symptoms such as babbling, drooling, and lapsing into semi-unconsciousness.

She was glad it was over, but it had stopped her from sleeping at night. Every time she tried to lie down, she would just imagine the night with him. Everything was coming back to her as the drug was wearing off. She had been given medication to increase brain activity and counteract any of the drugs negative affects on her neurological system. The more she took the medication Dr. Powers prescribed for her, the better she remembered—vividly.

They were not horrible memories. Matter of fact, they were all so beautiful and sweet. She was touched at how much love had really transpired between them and Thaddeus had held up his deal to the officers to make her unconscious experience bearable and pleasant. Yet, she could not forgive him. He knew she had not been in a willing state of consciousness, but allowed himself to make love to her when he knew everything from the beginning.

He had tried to come into contact with her. The roses, the cards, the poems, and the telephone calls: all of which she never accepted. He had tried to come by several times, but she specifically told the officers that guarded her door not to let him in. She wanted nothing to do with him *ever* again.

So why did she hurt so badly? Why did she feel so sad? She wondered all the time when she denied him to see her. Why did she want to make love to him over and over again? Dr. Powers told her she would have emotional attachment because of what was shared between them, but she shouldn't distinguished her need for companionship from what her fantasies were. Most time when he came to the hotel, she had a feeling the doctor did not care for Thaddeus and that he was putting a lot of things in her head to sway her from what she was really feeling. Yet sometimes, he did have a point. She could be mixing her emotions with what she wanted to be true. If she made love to him in reality maybe it wouldn't be the same as it was because she couldn't imagine feeling so good when she was alert and in her right mind. Her mind pondered these thoughts as she sat up at night flipping through the channels watching Matlock or Infomercials or watching the New Years celebration wondering whom was he kissing on midnight.

"Ms Patterson," Craig called out to her.

She knew the cops must have let him in. Sergeant Nolan had ordered she receive protection for two extra months after the trial and even surveillance until the end of the year. This had made testifying a little easier, but she still feared going out a little.

"How's it going?" he asked walking into the living room where she was knelt over her busted computer looking quite upset and sad.

"Not good, as you can see. They completely trashed my house, probably looking for the vials I took." She had turned all the evidence over to the police initially not wanting it as her responsibility anymore. "It's a good thing I backed up all my files and Sheila was helping me with billing and assigning work." Sheila had even done the transcribing for the Newman Enterprises Lyn assigned to the transcribing service; because Skye didn't want to even imagine doing anything for him if she didn't have to. The longer she disassociated herself from him the better she was able to sort out her emotions. "How's your arm?" she asked noting he was still sporting a sling for his arm, but no bandages. The bullet had shattered his shoulder, but with a lot of pins and steel the doctor's replaced the entire joint making it almost new.

"Great, matter of fact, I'll be back to work by the end of the year," he said very proudly, and then decided to get down to business. "Well, I have good news for you."

She stood up. "Should I sit down for this?"

"No, you're fine." He handed her an envelope from his inside jacket pocket. On the front was her name typed neatly. It was addressed from a law practice downtown.

Upon opening the envelope she gasped. "What is this?" she asked looking at the check for five hundred thousand dollars and some change.

"It's a bonus you could say. Remember that lawyer friend of mine who paid you a visit to help you cover your medical costs from what the medical center did to you?"

She nodded.

"Well he took it upon his liberty to fight the causes of all the women who were affected by these doctors and sued their estate. You'd already granted him permission to use your testimonies and name in his litigation with the doctor's lawyers, so he proceeded to win every suit for you. After taking out his cut, this was what was left for all the women divided up, from all three doctor's estates."

She sat down in her desk chair staring at all the zeros on the check. It was amazing and she couldn't believe it. "What about Dr. Carter?"

"His trial is coming up, for attempted murder, and GHB possession. He should get life or at least no parole for about fifteen years. The state plans to be hard to people involved in any GHB handling cases to send a message to all the ones that got away. Either way, he's destitute."

"It's all mine?"

"Yes, but the lawyer said if you didn't mind he took the liberty of putting aside the money already that you owe the IRS and at tax time he would deposit this amount into your account. He's also set up the services of a very impressive profiled investment clerk who is also an accountant who could rightly set you up for a very nice life. His card is in the envelope and he said if you felt comfortable enough to give him a call, he'll be waiting"

She was so shocked. Looking up at him through tear filled eyes, she tried to smile in appreciation, but was so flabbergasted smiling seemed complex. "Thank you so much." Standing up, she hugged him tightly.

He flushed from her appreciation through his somewhat dark brown sugared skin. "It's no problem. Unfortunately, it's not me who you should thank."

Just looking up into his eyes, she knew whom he wanted to say, but she had made him promise not to say that man's name in her presence if he wanted to speak with her. Thaddeus had tried to use Craig to get to her, but Craig didn't want to jeopardize the friendship he had grown to like with Skye and respected her wishes.

She moved away from him turning her back on him. "If I was a hateful person I would give it all back you know."

"Why? It's yours. It rightfully belongs to you. Thaddeus just got better and faster results because of his influence in certain places. He made sure all the other women and their families were paid off. You were a valuable key to all of this, and without you those women would have nothing."

She faced him. "Do I have to thank him personally then, or will you do it for me?"

"I could do it for you," he said reluctantly, "but I'd much rather you do it."

Skye knew she was acting silly. Good Lord, he was just a man and people had sex everyday. It should not bother her so much that she had experienced a good time, but it was. Maybe because she had never expected to enjoy sex after her awful memories of it when she was younger. "Would he like me to thank him personally?"

Craig smiled a beautiful cajoling smile meaning, 'yes.'

"Fine, I'll do it."

"Tonight at his place?"

It felt too soon, but she decided to go ahead and do it. "I will meet him a Fishbone's downtown restaurant. I think meeting Mr. Newman at an intimate place such as his apartment would not be appropriate and you can tell him I said so."

Craig nodded in agreement. "Don't let him get the upper hand, Skye." He bowed in consideration and she curtsied.

"You bet your broken arm I won't," she promised.

*   *   *

Dressed in a simple after five black dress of rayon that flowed down to her knees and some pleasant pumps she walked into Fishbone's restaurant feeling as if a million butterflies were in her stomach. The host greeted her at the door and she really wasn't sure what to say.

"Do you have reservations?" he asked.

"N-No," she said nervously nothing that it was rather quiet and she didn't see anyone around. This was strange for this very popular restaurant on a Thursday night. "I'm meeting a Mr. Newman."

"Ah!" he said excitedly. "Please come this way, he has been eagerly expecting you." He led her through the restaurant, which was empty to a cubbyhole on a raised dais. Thaddeus was seated there in a nice gray Louis Vitton suit. When they approached he stood and flashed a heart-dropping smile that could melt ice.

Lowering her eyes, she decided not to show her emotions just about yet. The attendant left them alone after taking her coat and getting her order for a nice white wine.

After seating her, he sat across from her feeling a bit hesitant as well, but she didn't notice because she was too involved with her own emotions.

"You look beautiful," he complimented her.

"Thank you, but I didn't come here to get smoke blown up my butt, Mr. Newman. I would like to get to the issues at hand." She paused as a waiter delivered their drinks. He'd ordered a club soda too uptight to drink any alcohol. He took the liberty of ordering their food for her, which she didn't mind and once the waiter was gone, she continued to speak.

"I'm upset with you. Not because we made love. Remembering it all I could sense you were very attracted to me and that there was a lot of emotions and resistance to you."

"I am still very attracted to you, Skye, much more. I want-"

She cut him off. "Please let me finish, Mr. Newman."

He nodded in acquiesce.

"I'm upset with you because when you knew, you could have come over and let me know, you didn't and it caused a lot of mental stress upon me before and after the incident. You deceived me. You could have stopped at any moment even after I arrived that night and gave me the sleeping serum." While she waited for trial, Dr. Powers tried to make her believe she disputed to herself, she confirmed the serum with Sergeant Nolan. "You didn't and there is no way to take back the nights, and there is no way to apologize for what could have been a horrible experience for me."

He knew this and it showed so clearly in his eyes as to how sorry he was that she just wanted to reach over and kiss him to let him know everything was okay, but she wanted to also let him stew about it too, because the attention he poured upon her for his actions were just the sweetest.

When he was sure she was done, so he could speak, Thaddeus chose his words carefully and allowed himself to breath himself to calmness as he spoke to her. "I can never apologize enough for what I did, but just knowing I was going to have you made all reason come to a hold. I wanted you and when the opportunity came that I could have you, I took it, because I want it more than life itself." He gently took her stiff hands in his. "I've cursed, bullied and argued with myself over these last months, over what I did to you, Skye and I know there is no way in the world you could possibly forgive me, but I've come to realize a thing or two about myself and us."

She raised a deep honey brow waiting for him to continued as he pause to get a drink to wet his throat.

"I would do anything in this world to have you close to me. Not just your body but also your mind, your soul . . . your heart. You've come to mean a great deal to me than just a case I worked on with Craig and more than just a friend. You've come to mean a world only you and I could share that would make us happy. Even though you weren't willing you were doing what your conscious wanted to do in that situation. You told me. You wanted me, just as much as I wanted you and I know you cannot deny it, but I hope with everything that has happened, I haven't ruined it all for you and I." He leaned in close to her. "Have I?"

Her eyes lowered to their joined hands, then raised slowly to meet his. "No you haven't," she admitted honestly. "I can't stop thinking about you and . . . I do want you in my life."

He smiled almost victorious, but quenched his emotions knowing he should not show his triumph yet. "I want you in my life as well, Skye. More than ever, I've come to realize I don't want to spend another day with you."

She lowered her head to hide the joy that was appearing. His hand softly caressed her cheek then gently nudged up her chin until she was looking into his eyes. He smiled wonderfully. "I've waited so long to see you show me some joy. Let me show you more for the rest of your life, Skye. Let me be that man you walk down the aisle with."

She couldn't help herself. Releasing his hands, she cupped his face and kissed him. His response was immediate and lingered until they knew what they wanted right then.

He could see the heat in her eyes and suggested with a lot of caution, "We could go to a room at the Athenaeum behind the restaurant that I have for my out of town guest and have the food delivered."

Skye frowned, worrying Thaddeus a bit. "Are you always so prepared?"

"When dealing with you, yes."

"You know I just came to thank you for the wonderful check I received today."

"Are you thanking me now, or did you want to thank me in the room?"

She smiled wickedly. "Why don't I thank you at breakfast?"

Thaddeus smiled in understanding. It would be a wonderful night for the both of them sharing love beyond compare.

Chapter 21

Skye felt herself come awake, but she didn't want to open her eyes. She didn't want to wake up in her bed all alone like the last time of having a beautiful night of love had happened to her. Yet the most astounding stimulation encompassed her body from head to toe. The powerful fervencies were coming from her groin and they were getting stronger until she allowed herself to explode releasing a sexually gratified whimper never opening her eyes the entire time.

"I know you're awake," Thaddeus said anxiously.

She gasped feeling his hot mouth on her breast coaxing the dark tip to hardness, and then she purred in pleasure loving the sensations overwhelming her body.

"You don't have to open your eyes," he whispered moving on top of her. She could feel his stiffness finding her moistness and entered her to the hilt. His groaned joined hers as satisfaction covered his body as well to feel her so responsive to his ministrations. "I know what you think." The tip of his tongue traced erotically around the edge of her passion filled lips from one corner to the next at the top, then did the same at the bottom.

"Do you?" she asked still keeping her eyes closed.

"Yes, you think this is a dream still and if you open your eyes I will go away, but it's not going to happen, because I know I'm not dreaming. I'll prove it to you."

"How? Are you going to pinch me?" She giggled breathlessly, but he moved in a circular motion and her laughter immediately turned to moans of pleasure. He stopped before he got carried away wanting too much to enjoy the powerful emotions, which made his body screamed for more.

"I'm going to make love to you until you open your eyes and convince you it's not a dream anymore."

"I'm pretty stubborn," she teased. For that she received another circular motion from him that sent more sensations through her making her gasp and cling to him for more.

In her ear he whispered, "If it takes all day, I'm game."

That sent warm chills down her spine. She was definitely game to that. They made love until nightfall enjoying every moment of it.

* * *

When she awoke, she felt a slight soreness in her throat. She knew this was from screaming mercy to let him know she was truly convinced a man who could make love all day could be no dream. The room was filled with lit candles and there was a note attached to a rose on the pillow beside her.

DON'T LEAVE! HAD TO RUN AN ERRAND BACK TO MY PLACE. WILL BE RIGHT BACK WITH SOME THING FOR YOU TO WEAR.

TN

She like when he signed his initials. Putting the letter down, she got up and refreshed herself in the bathroom. Skye was starving, so she ordered dinner for the both of them with more white champagne. While she waited she called Sheila then check her answering machine using the phone beside the bed wrapped up in a beautiful white hotel terry-cloth robe.

The computer on her voicemail spoke in a monotonous tone, "You have one new message." It was from today's date.

A rather nervous deep voice came on next, which surprise her. "Hi Ms Patterson, I was . . . well my name is Thomas Blair and I was informed you lived at this phone number. I'm in town looking for you because . . . well-ehh . . . because I believed you are my daughter . . . I would like to speak with you regarding this issue, please. I am staying at the Athenaeum Hotel in downtown Detroit, suite four-twenty-one. No matter the hour, please call or come by. I am very eager to meet you."

She hung up stunned again. This was just too much to adjust to in one day.

"I brought a nightgown and robe for you to . . ." Thaddeus walked in at that moment, but his words trailed off as he noticed how spaced out she looked at that moment.

"Are you okay?" he asked sitting next to her putting the bag down with the clothes.

She composed herself, yet her thoughts ran wild.

He saw she seemed distracted by something. "Well, I guess I shouldn't ask you something about now since your mind is a mile away." He moved in front of her kneeling while studying her face.

"What? . . . No, I'm listening. What did you want?" She tired her best to give him her full attention.

He reached in his breast pocket and pulled out a velvet ring box. Her heart began to beat erratically as he opened the box to reveal a two-carat heart shaped ring. "Would you marry me, Skye?"

Tears welled up in her eyes and she put her hands up to cover her mouth.

When she didn't respond immediately he said, "I was think-ing of going to Lake Tahoe for a weekend. My mother wouldn't have time to attend and since you have no family, I didn't think a large ceremony would be on your mind, but we can have one later on if you wish. A double ceremony can be arranged, but I just wanted you to be mine as soon as possible."

How many times had she dreamed of this? She asked herself. Lord, the man was phenomenal! "Yes," she mumbled through her hands.

"What was that?" he said pulling her left hand down to un-cover half of her face.

"Yes," she whimpered as he slipped the ring on her finger.

He kissed her in appreciation. "I'll make everyday a dream come true, Skye, I promise." He kissed her again then once more— longer, stirring his manhood to response.

There was a knock at the door.

"We should get it," she said.

"No we shouldn't. Are you expecting company?" he asked annoyed someone was bothering them.

"Just room service."

He sighed and allowed her to get up. "Put the nightgown and robe on, then we'll have dinner on the balcony. It's a nice warm night."

She agreed as he headed for the front door, closing the bedroom door for her privacy.

Opening the hotel room door, he was surprised to see Thomas standing there. "Hi Thomas, what are you doing in town?"

"I've been trying to call you for the last two months. I have good news."

"I've been pursuing a big project and hadn't returned anyone's calls. How did you know I was here?" he asked suspiciously.

"I saw you in the lobby and asked the desk clerk what room you were in. I didn't know you stayed here or were you visiting? Did I interrupt you?"

"I've been here for a couple of nights, but please come in. I'd like you to meet my fiancé."

He stepped into the room. "So you've figured out who you want to be with?"

"Well funny you should say that, because the Case and the woman were one in the same."

Thomas gave him a confused look.

Thaddeus laughed. "I know you don't understand, but I've got an earful for you. I'll tell you everything much later. While we are waiting for her, what good news did you have to tell me?"

"You know I've spent almost the last year searching for my daughter with the clues her mother gave me. I've been on so many wild goose chases I almost gave up until I found her. Well, Detective Heart found her and you'll never believe it, but my daughter lives here in Detroit and she runs her own business." He sounded so proud.

Thaddeus was honestly elated for his friend. His long search was over. They hugged to celebrate the joyous occasion. "What's her name? Have you seen her? How does she look?"

Thomas laughed loving the enthusiasm Thaddeus expressed reminding him of his own self when Detective Heart told him about the positive findings. "It's all so much to tell, but I called her this afternoon. She hasn't called back, but that hasn't discouraged me. I did go over to her home and she wasn't there. I left a note on the door though, so I'm sure she will call me soon."

"So what is her name? Is it still the same?" Thaddeus asked eagerly.

"No- No. She was only taught a partial of her first name and given the permanent last name of the first people who adopted her, but died shortly afterwards. It's Skye Patterson-"

"Yes," the woman answered stepping out the bedroom door.

Thaddeus eyes went wide. He was struck speechless as he began to put all the pieces together. Talk about six degrees of separation.

Thomas turned and his jaw dropped. He would have sworn on everything he was seeing Agatha walking towards him. The young woman smiled shyly and introduced herself because both men seemed awed by her. She could excuse Thaddeus since he was in love with her, but this older man was looking at her as if she were a ghost.

"Agatha," he whispered.

"No," Thaddeus said realizing Skye and her deceased mother must have looked very much alike. He probably would have put two and two together earlier if he had went with Thomas to the estate Agatha had left Skye over in Europe, but he had become too involved in getting Skye back to accompany Thomas across the sea this past month. "It's not, Thomas."

Thomas cleared his throat recalling the name the detective had given him. "Skye? Skye Patterson?" This was why Thaddeus had been so shocked.

She nodded and held her hand out to be shaken.

The man looked down at her hand, then her whole body from head to toe, making her feel very self-conscious. Suddenly, he pulled her into a bear hug she thought for sure would suffocate her. She gave Thaddeus, who looked awed, a look of confusion.

When Thomas pulled away, he apologized wiping some tears from his eyes, as she looked perplexed. "I'm truly sorry, my dear, I just couldn't help myself."

"I have that effect on men," she replied quite surly.

He chuckled amazed she even sounded like Agatha a little. "I must introduce myself first. Skye Patterson, I'm your father, Thomas Blair."

She remembered the name from the answering machines then the letters she had typed for Thaddeus. "You're my father?" she exclaimed.

"Yes, Yes!" he said with a lot of relief. "I've been searching for you for years and years, until your mother died, I had no place to really know where you were. She died a year ago almost and she carried the secret of what she did with you to her grave leaving me all the information in a letter." He produced the paper as he spoke handing the letter to her. "You look almost like her. You're more beautiful than I would ever imagine."

Skye was speechless. She couldn't believe what this man had told her. The man she had always dreamed of knowing was standing in front of her now. Standing next to the man she would be with for the rest of her life, then back at the man responsible for bringing her in the world. She was overwhelmed with emotions and didn't know if after going through an immense amount of trauma in the past months if she could cope with knowing the truth about herself.

Thaddeus could see her knees becoming weak and helped her to the couch.

"How did you know her Thaddeus?" Thomas asked.

"We are getting married. This is who I was telling you about."

"The case and employee?"

"Yes."

He looked a bit upset and confused.

"We'll tell you everything later. Right now she is my concern."

"I think not. I've waited too long to spoil her rotten. She is my concern until you are married."

Skye looked hopelessly from one man to another. 'He does have a point Thaddeus. We've just met each other and I should give him some time."

"I have waited far too long to have you, Skye. I don't intend to give you up to another man. I don't care if he is like a father to me."

Skye looked at him deeply. "Thaddeus, what we share will be for a lifetime and you know it as much as I do, but this is my father." She took Thomas hand. "A man I've waited all my life to meet. Please."

Skye was the world to him and he didn't want to share her, but this was something she wanted and Thomas wanted to spoil her as much as Thaddeus. He had a feeling this little lady was going to wrap two very powerful men around her finger. He nodded his consent as much as he hated doing it.

Thomas sat down beside her. "Why don't we fly to Florida immediately?" he suggested. "I'll help prepare for the wedding. You can have it down there at my home."

She looked at Thaddeus for approval. He nodded again and even smiled seeing how much joy it brought her. "This is the happiest day of my life," she told them both and threw her arms around her father's neck. "Thank you."

"No, thank Thaddeus because it was his hard work, determination, and connections that helped me to find you."

She turned towards Thaddeus and hugged him kissing his check. "Thank you."

"You've said thanks enough when you said yes to marrying me, woman. I am thankful to have you in my life."

"As am I." She pressed her sultry lips against his. "You've made all my dreams come true, Thaddeus."